# I'd Sooner Have Love

*Janet Lee Barton*

*Heartsong Presents*

To my Lord and Savior for showing me the way,
to my family for their constant loving support,
and to all my readers—I'm blessed.

A note from the Author:
*I love to hear from my readers! You may correspond with
me by writing:*

**Janet Lee Barton**
**Author Relations**
**PO Box 721**
**Uhrichsville, OH 44683**

**ISBN 978-1-61626-335-5**

**I'D SOONER HAVE LOVE**

All scripture quotations are taken from the King James Version of the Bible.

All of the characters and events in this book are fictitious. Any resem-
blance to actual persons, living or dead, or to actual events is purely
coincidental.

*Our mission is to publish and distribute inspirational products offering
exceptional value and biblical encouragement to the masses.*

PRINTED IN THE U.S.A.

## "Ready, Faith?" Ben called from outside the wagon.

"I'm ready." Hope had cleaned up after breakfast but still was finished dressing long before Faith, and now everyone waited for her. Faith hurried out and took Ben's helping hand to climb down.

"Are you alright, sis? You were awful quiet at breakfast."

"I'm fine." And she would be. It was a beautiful Sunday, and she would think on all the good things in her life and rejoice in them.

When she saw Gabe striding over in their direction, her heart warmed because he was taking her up on the invitation to join them.

"Thought I'd join you in church this morning," he said.

Her heart did a triple flip as he smiled at her, and Faith was glad when Ben answered for her.

"We'd be glad for you to join us. It's the best way to start a week that I know of."

Gabe only nodded as he fell into step beside them. Faith had wondered if he would ever go to church with them, and now that he was, her heart felt about ready to burst with joy.

Faith never thought any other man would be able to claim her heart after her Noah, but Gabe Logan seemed to be making his own place. And she couldn't let that happen. It would only serve to bring heartache—for she would never marry again.

**JANET LEE BARTON** and her husband, Dan, have recently moved to Oklahoma and feel blessed to have at least one daughter and her family living nearby. Janet loves being able to share her faith and love of the Lord through her writing. She's very happy that the kind of romances the Lord has called her to write can be read by and shared with women of all ages.

Books by Janet Lee Barton

**HEARTSONG PRESENTS**
HP434—Family Circle
HP532—A Promise Made
HP562—Family Ties
HP623—A Place Called Home
HP644—Making Amends
HP689—Unforgettable
HP710—To Love Again
HP730—With Open Arms
HP745—Family Reunion
HP759—Stirring Up Romance
HP836—A Love for Keeps
HP852—A Love All Her Own
HP852—A Love to Cherish

Don't miss out on any of our super romances. Write to us at the following address for information on our newest releases and club information.

Heartsong Presents Readers' Service
PO Box 721
Uhrichsville, OH 44683

Or visit www.heartsongpresents.com

## one

Faith Anderson watched her brother, Ben, crack the whip over the team and give a flick of his wrist to the reins. They lurched forward and were on their way.

Failing to stem the excitement bubbling up inside, Faith leaned over the seat of the wagon and looked ahead and behind them at what seemed an endless procession of wagons all heading in the same direction. She turned to look through the cover to the back of their wagon, where her nephew and niece were waving to the people behind them. All were leaving Arkansas City, heading toward the new lands that would be opened up on the twenty-second.

Relieved to be on their way, Faith let out a deep breath and smiled at her brother. "Do you think there's going to be enough land for everyone, Ben?"

Ben shrugged and grinned at her. "I don't know, but there sure better be. A lot of folks are counting on it—including us." He was silent for a few moments, his brow furrowed, which meant he was worrying about something.

It didn't take long to find out what was on his mind. Her big brother turned to look at her. "I do wonder if I should have left you, Hope, and Matt to come later though."

Faith shook her head vehemently. "No. The trains were so booked up, it would have been late afternoon before we could

5

catch one—if then. It's better if we stay together—you know it is." She grinned at him and raised an eyebrow. "Besides, it's too late now. We're out ahead of a lot of those wagons, Ben. We'll be all right."

"We're going to have to be, Faith. There's nothing to go back to."

His tone was grim, but he was right. Ben had been a widower for more than two years, and her husband, Noah, had died the year before. Even if she'd had something to go back to, Faith didn't want to.

She'd never been able to provide Noah's parents with grandchildren, and they had made life miserable for her ever since he passed away. Hard as she tried, she didn't think she'd ever forget Noah's mother saying, "You only married him for our money, and he was never really happy married to you." Faith couldn't be more relieved to be away from them. She was just thankful that her husband had provided enough for her to make a new life somewhere else.

Ben cracked the whip again, but it did little good. It had rained recently, and the road was muddy, causing some wagons to bog down. More than once that morning, they'd come to a stop because of trouble in front of them.

Ben and Matt joined several others to help a man two wagons ahead. When they got the wagon moving again, Ben hurried back, and they were able to travel several hours before slowing down once more. Once they crossed the Arkansas River Bridge, they felt they were well on their way. As the prairie schooners spread out over the grassland, it looked like a sea of white. "I've never seen anything like this," Ben said.

Faith's throat clogged up just thinking about so many people traveling together, all wanting the same thing. To build a new life in a new place.

She and the children took turns sitting up front, waving at people alongside or behind them. It was a long day, but by the time they reached camp at Willow Springs that night, anticipation flowed from one campfire to the next.

Traveling alongside the river gave them access to water and made for a good place to set up camp for the night. After eating supper and meeting some of their fellow settlers, Faith sensed excitement was running high. It was both comforting and frightening to know so many people were headed in the same direction to claim land. Some were looking for enough land for a ranch or farm. Others just wanted a place in town to start up businesses.

The Millers, whose wagon was to the left of theirs, were going to open a restaurant. "I think we're goin' to do right fine," Mr. Miller said. "There's bound to be lots of single men in the new settlement, and they'll need fed. My wife is one of the best cooks I know. We can't help but do well."

If Mr. Miller's girth was any indication, Mrs. Miller was indeed a good cook. Faith had never thought of opening a restaurant. It would be a big undertaking, to be sure.

"We're hoping to do well," Mrs. Miller said, more modestly. She was a sweet woman who seemed full of energy and a positive outlook. "With things still so bad up in Kansas, we decided we don't have much to lose."

"That seems to be what most people heading to Guthrie are saying," Ben said.

The couple on the other side of them, the Johnsons, just wanted a home in town and would decide what to do later. Faith couldn't blame them. She wasn't sure about her future either. All she knew was that she was finally free from her husband's uncaring, dictating parents. She'd look to the Lord to guide her in this new land.

૨૦

The next day, Captain Hayes and his troops led them out again, but the excitement of the day turned to frustration when they got to the Salt Fork of the Arkansas River. Normally easy to cross, but now in flood stage from recent rains, the river presented a real problem for the settlers.

"How are we going to get across, Aunt Faith?" Hope asked while they sat waiting and watching as Ben and Matt went to see what they could do.

"I don't know, Hope." Faith didn't want to show how frightened she was at the prospect of crossing the tumultuous water, but she needed to prepare her niece. "I'm sure they'll find a way, but it's not going to be easy."

Several men had been sent ahead to make a temporary bridge, but it was hastily built and rickety and deemed too dangerous to use for crossing the rampaging water. An old ferryboat was put into service, and some settlers set about to build their own rafts, but Faith thought the rafts looked much too flimsy to carry a wagon across. She could only pray that they would hold up. Finally, it was decided that the four-span Howe trestle railroad bridge farther down the river would be the best answer to crossing the Salt Fork. But they ran into more problems when the officials there refused to allow it, wanting to charge for transporting the settlers' belongings instead. Faith feared a fight was going to break out when some of the settlers demanded the use of the bridge while others suggested that the tracks be torn up so that trains couldn't use it and others suggested tearing down a building to get enough lumber to cover the bridge.

"What's happening? Are we going to be able to cross here, or do we have to find another way?" Faith asked Ben as he and Matt came back to the wagon.

"Captain Hayes telegraphed the superintendent of the Santa Fe, telling him that he would not be responsible for their property unless the railroad allowed the settlers to cross on the bridge," Ben said. "Finally, he was given the go ahead to do whatever was needed to keep the railroad intact. The captain ordered planking at the Ponca Depot to be taken down and laid over the railroad ties across the bridge. It's going to be awhile yet before we can cross. And we're going to have to be lighter when we do. We'll have to unload some things here."

Ben and Matt pitched in and helped with the tracks while Faith and Hope began to pull out what they could bear to part with. Tears in their eyes, they managed to unpack the small sideboard that had belonged to Hope's mother, then pull it out of the wagon and onto the riverbank. They removed a small crate of dishes Faith could remember from her childhood and another of silverware that had been in Hope's family for years. But things were replaceable; they knew that all too well. It was people who couldn't be restored, and they were blessed to get across when they did.

Still, crossing the bridge wasn't easy, and Faith was beholden to the man who helped Ben get their wagon across. He was tall and handsome, his dark brown hair matching his piercing eyes.

When they arrived safely on the other side, she thanked him for his help.

He tipped his hat. "You're welcome, ma'am. I hope y'all find a place and have a safe trip."

With that, he was on his horse and gone. Just him. No wagon and no family. Perhaps he'd left them to come later and was heading to claim land for a family. Or perhaps he was alone—

"That was sure nice of that man," Ben jumped up onto the wagon seat after tying his horse, Rusty, to the back.

"Yes, it was." Faith watched the stranger ride away until she could see him no more. "It was very nice."

She wondered if they'd ever see him again.

※

Gabe Logan was glad he'd been able to help the young couple cross the Salt Ford. He'd stayed to help when he saw one wagon floating down the river after trying to cross the temporary bridge instead of waiting to use the railroad bridge. He hoped the young couple made it the rest of the way.

Going back and forth from one side of the river to the other, Gabe helped several other travelers cross before finally leaving the river and heading toward the front of the line. After awhile, hunger had him pulling out some jerky and hardtack from his saddlebag. It was getting tiresome, but it put a stop to the growling of his stomach for the moment.

He kept thinking about the first family he'd helped. The young, red-headed woman sure was nice when she thanked him. She was pretty, too, with the bluest eyes he'd ever seen and that bright hair curling out from under her bonnet.

She didn't look old enough to be the mother of the girl and boy who were with her. Maybe they were her siblings. Something about them all had him feeling lonelier tonight than he'd been in a very long time. Maybe he'd run into them again one day. He wouldn't count on it though.

Gabe tried to put thoughts of them out of his head as he mounted his horse and nudged him into a run. He wanted to get to the front of the line as fast as he could.

# two

On Easter Sunday, the night before the run, Faith couldn't quite believe they'd made it to the Oklahoma district line in preparation for the next day. If she'd known what they were up against when they'd left Arkansas City three days earlier, she might have tried to talk her brother out of going. But no. Faith wanted this new start as badly as Ben did.

Still, it was most likely a good thing she'd been ignorant of the river crossings ahead or the number of people heading toward the same place. One thing she did know. She would have never made it across the Cimarron River without her brother in charge, and they might not have made it even then, if not for the help of that handsome stranger.

While Ben and Matt went to fetch water at the river, Faith finished cleaning up after supper and made sure the supplies were secured to the wagon. She left the pot of coffee on the fire, thinking Ben would probably want a cup when he got back to camp.

This day had seemed much longer than the day before, and she was exhausted. She'd call it a night when Ben and Matt returned, for they'd be up early readying everything for the final run to Guthrie. Thirteen-year-old Hope had already gone to bed and was sleeping soundly. She'd walked alongside the wagon most of the day and then helped with supper. She'd been quieter than usual after they'd crossed the Salt Fork, and Faith knew that leaving some of her mother's things behind had been very difficult for her.

11

Faith took a seat on one of the stools Ben had placed near the fire and looked up at the star-laden sky. It was beautiful country. Large cottonwoods shaded the rivers; the land looked untouched and fertile. The sunsets and sunrises were something to behold. It was going to be different from Wichita, that was for sure, but at least she wasn't alone.

She bowed her head and sent up a silent prayer. *Lord, thank You for seeing us across that river safely today. That was a mighty scary ride, but You were with us, and we made it here. Please help us get to Guthrie and find a good lot. And Lord, please help me and Ben guide Hope and Matt through this difficult time for us all. I know they miss their mama something awful—just like I miss my Noah. But we know they are in a better place, and that gives us a measure of comfort. Please help us all to look to You to guide us in this new land. In Jesus' name I pray. Amen.*

The Lord had brought them this far; He'd see they found a claim. Faith was sure of it.

❧

Ben had been doing a lot of thinking while he and Matt were down at the creek. He worried that they might not find a claim the next day. So many people were in this camp alone, but what about all the others coming in from different directions? How many more could there be? Thousands, probably.

At the creek, he found several other men discussing their fears. Some of them were talking about going to the front of the line and letting their families come at their own pace in the wagons. Ben was beginning to think he should do the same thing.

"You really think it's going to be that hard to get a claim?" he asked one of the older men.

"I've heard that people have been sneaking in for months.

Son, we'll be lucky if there's anything left between here and Guthrie," a man who'd introduced himself as Richard Lambert said.

"I been hearin' the same thing," another man said. "Some of these people have relatives who've already been in and wrote home about it. I'm goin' to the front of the line. Better that than have no place to call home by the time my wagon gets there."

"Well, I'm heading toward the front of the line when I get back to camp," a man who'd introduced himself as Charles Morgan said. "I can have a lot claimed long before my family catches up with me, and my wife wants a lot in town."

Seemed everyone was worried about the same thing—by the time the wagons got to Guthrie and the surrounding area, there wouldn't be any land or city lots left to choose. Surely most of that was rumor. Ben hoped so. He'd hate to think he had brought Faith and the children on a wild goose chase. He wasn't sure what the next day held, but he wanted it to end with a lot or land—something to call home for his children and his sister.

He and Matt filled their pails and headed back toward camp. "Son, I'm thinking I might go on ahead tomorrow. If I do, you'll help Faith get into Guthrie, won't you?"

Fourteen-year-old Matt grinned from ear to ear. "You'd trust me to do that?"

"Well of course I will. You are near a man now. You've helped me in the fields. You can handle the team almost as well as I can." That was a bit of an exaggeration, but the boy needed all the confidence Ben could give him. "Besides, if I go on first, you won't have to run full out with the team and wagon. It'll be safer for you all. I don't want to chance something happening to any of you."

"You're goin' to have to convince Aunt Faith of that, Papa. She'll say we'd be safer with you along. She thinks I'm still just a kid."

"I'll do my best to convince her she's wrong." Ben chuckled. "Let's get this water back to camp, and I'll tell her what I have in mind."

"She isn't going to like it."

"I know. But I think it's the only way we have a chance of getting land tomorrow. She'll agree." He hoped.

❧

When Faith opened her eyes, her brother and nephew were smiling at her. She stood and stretched. "I was just thanking the good Lord for safe travel."

"He did get us all here in one piece." Ben said as he and Matt emptied the water pails into the barrel tied to the wagon and came over to join her at the fire. "We need to pray He does the same tomorrow. Is there any coffee left?"

Faith shook the pot she'd set off to the side of the campfire. "Yes. I was keeping it warm, but it might be a bit on the strong side."

"It's okay."

She poured him a cup.

"Can I have some, too?" Matt asked

Faith raised an eyebrow. "Won't it keep you awake?"

"Nah. It won't."

"He'll be fine, Faith. He's growing up, you know."

She looked at her young nephew, who was taller than she was, and sighed. Matt brought back a cup and handed it to her with a grin. She poured him some of the strong liquid.

"I just hope you get to sleep after drinking it." She knew he'd never tell her if it did keep him awake. But Ben was right. Matt was growing up, and she needed to remember it.

Sometimes she treated her nephew as if he were still a little boy, but he was quickly growing into a young man and—

"Faith?" Ben broke into her thoughts. "Faith, I've decided to go to the front of the line. I'm sure my horse is fast as any out here, and the sooner I get there, the better chance I'll have of finding us a good lot."

"Ben! I don't want you to go ahead. We need to stay together. Something might happen—"

"Faith, I've been hearing talk. The wagon only goes so fast. You know what my horse can do. If I can get there ahead of you, Matt, and Hope, I can have us a lot staked out when you get there. I'm really afraid that if I don't go in first, there won't be any land left to claim."

Faith heard what he was saying, and in her heart, she knew he was right. Hadn't she been worrying about the very same thing? But she was afraid. She'd never handled the wagon on her own, and she had Matt and Hope to think about.

"Sis, it's going to be all right. I've taught Matt to drive the team."

"Matt? No. I can drive it. I have. Just not—"

"I want to drive the team, Aunt Faith. I'll be careful. I promise." Matt looked at her, his eyes big and begging her to let him be a man. "Please? If we get in trouble or you think you can do a better job, I'll hand over the reins. I promise."

Faith sighed. How that boy could tug at her heartstrings. "I just don't know—"

"Faith, he's helped me in the fields these last few years. He'll be fine. Just don't worry about getting in a hurry. You won't have to rush if I go ahead, and it will be a safer trip than if we're fighting to get ahead of everyone else. You know it will."

Faith couldn't argue about that. But she'd felt secure with Ben guiding them. Now he was asking her not only to make the rest of the trip without him but also to trust Matt to get them there.

She looked from her brother to his son, the expressions in their eyes. . .hopeful from Matt, pleading from Ben. She sighed and gave a slight nod. "All right. You go on ahead. I'll let Matt start out. But I'm not promising that he can take us all the way. Just start out, okay?"

Matt grinned and nodded, and Ben hugged her. "This is for the best, sis. It really is."

She hugged him back and sighed. Much as she hated to admit it, he was right. "When are you going to go to the front of the line?"

"Tonight," Ben answered. "Some of the other men are going to do the same thing. We need to get into position as soon as we can."

"But won't tomorrow morning be soon enough? We can't move until noon."

"I know, but I don't want to have to fight for a good position in the morning. It's every man for himself tomorrow."

What he said made sense, and Faith knew it. She nodded. "Well, let's get you ready to go."

While he saddled his horse, Faith tied up some hardtack, jerky, and coffee in a handkerchief and handed it to him, along with a small pot and a tin cup.

Ben slid the packet into his saddlebag and tied the pot and cup to it. He tied a bedroll and a few other things he thought he might need onto the other side of the saddle. "That should do me for tonight. We'll all be together tomorrow evening," he assured her.

Faith tried not to tear up. "Let me get Hope, and we'll say a prayer."

Ben shook his head. "Let her sleep. No need to have her

wake up and start worrying."

He reached out to Faith and to Matt, who grabbed his hands. They all bowed their heads while Ben prayed. "Dear Lord, please watch over Faith, Matt, and Hope tomorrow. Please give them guidance as they make their way into Guthrie, and let them get there safely. Please be with me, Father. Please guide me, see me safely there, and help me to find the right land or lot for us. Please let us all be reunited tomorrow. We thank You for seeing us this far, and we trust You to see us the rest of the way. In Jesus' name we pray. Amen."

Ben hugged them both and mounted the sorrel he trusted to get him to Guthrie in one piece and as fast as possible. He looked down at Faith and Matt. "Take care."

He flicked the reins and walked Rusty out of the campsite. It was dark, but the moon was bright, and Faith could see him begin to gallop toward the front of the line. She fought the fear that washed over her and the tears that threatened to fall.

Matt must have sensed her mood, for he put an arm around her shoulders and gave her a quick hug. "He'll be all right, and so will we, Aunt Faith. By this time tomorrow night, we'll all be settling in."

Reminding herself that she was trusting the Lord to see them through, she prayed, *Dear Lord, please watch over us all.*

## three

The sun was just setting when Gabe Logan made it up to the front of the line and found a spot to set up camp. He was about as ready as a body could be for the run the next day. He looked up at the night sky and took a swallow of the coffee he'd put on to boil while he set out his bedroll. These were the same stars and moon he'd seen countless times in Kansas, but somehow out here they seemed brighter and larger.

He'd met several of the men who'd come up to the front line to be part of the first wave of land seekers to take off when the shot was fired the next day. Some were young and cocky, others a little older and wiser, but all were anxious to find a place to call their own.

As he listened to talk around the campfire, Gabe didn't think anyone could be looking forward to making a new start more than he was. The last year had been a nightmare, and he just wanted to put it behind him.

The troops kept a close eye on the line, and as far as Gabe could see no one was crazy enough to try to run past them here, but he was sure some out there would find a place to try. As for him—he wasn't about to get on the wrong side of the law—not after the last few months.

Gabe thought he recognized the man he'd helped earlier in the day when he rode up to the group near the front of the line where most of the horse riders had gone.

"Got room for one more up here?" the newcomer asked.

"Sure. Long as you don't take up much space," a man

named Lambert said with a chuckle.

"I'll try not to, sir." The man dismounted and hitched his horse to a nearby bush along with several others.

"Come on over to the fire and warm yourself. These nights are still a bit nippy," an older man named Jed Green said.

Gabe was drinking his coffee when the man approached the fire. He acknowledged him with a slight nod. Maybe it hadn't been his family whose wagon he'd helped get unstuck. It sure looked like him, though, and as he came closer, Gabe was sure it was the same man.

"I'm Ben Thompson, and I didn't have a chance to thank you for helping me and my family the other day." The newcomer held out his hand. "I'm glad to have a chance to now."

So it had been his family. Gabe Logan was glad he'd been able to help the young couple when they'd gotten bogged down just outside of Guthrie. For some reason, he'd been thinking about them ever since. That auburn hair and the bluest eyes he'd ever seen were hard to forget. He kept thinking that she didn't look old enough to be the mother of the girl and boy who were with her. Maybe they were her siblings and not the couple's children. Anyway, Thompson was a lucky man to have a family like that. He took Ben's hand and shook it. "Gabe Logan's my name. I'm pleased to meet you. I was glad to be of help. You goin' in ahead of your family like the rest of these men?"

Ben nodded. "It seemed the best plan. That old wagon is a good one, but by the time it makes it to Guthrie, there might not be any lots to be had."

"Ain't that the truth," one old-timer said, right before he spit into the fire. "My wife practically pushed me out of our wagon. Course she can handle that team 'bout as good as I can."

They all seemed to agree that it was best to go in ahead

of their families and find some land to call their own by the next night.

"You on your own?" Ben asked Gabe as he put down his bedroll in an open area not too far from the fire.

"Yes." But he didn't elaborate. That would entail thinking about the past—something he didn't want to do.

"It's probably easier that way," Ben said. "At least you don't have to worry about leaving them out here to make the run without you."

Gabe supposed that was one way to think about it. He just wasn't sure he'd be lookin' at it that way. He was thankful when the conversation around the fire turned to the next day and the excitement of the race to find a home. It was late when they all quieted down for the night, and Gabe tried not to think of Ben and his wife and the young'uns traveling with him. He just hoped the man knew how blessed he was to have such a family.

a

The coffee didn't seem to keep Matt awake. He snored most of the night. Faith was glad that Hope had gone to bed earlier; otherwise she most likely never would have gone to sleep.

Faith probably wouldn't have slept much even had Matt's snoring ceased. She'd tossed and turned, thinking about the next morning. She'd never felt more weight on her shoulders than she did at that moment.

Finally at dawn, she got up and started a fire to make coffee before starting breakfast for Matt and Hope. Another woman just a few wagons down waved at Faith and moments later came over with two cups of coffee. She handed one to Faith. "I thought you might like a cup while you wait for yours to boil."

Faith gladly took it. "Thank you."

"I saw your man ride out last night, too. My husband went to the front right before he did." She held out her hand. "I'm Rose Lambert."

Faith shook her hand. "I'm Faith Anderson. That was my older brother who rode out. He thinks it will be better to go in ahead of us. He's most likely right, but I'm sure nervous about today." She brought out two stools so that they could sit by the fire. Faith pulled her shawl closer to ward off the morning chill. "Please, join me."

"Don't mind if I do." Mrs. Lambert took a seat. "I know how you feel. But this way we don't have to get in a terrible hurry. That's when the accidents happen and it's unsafe. If we just let our teams take us at their own pace, we'll be safer."

Faith nodded. "That's what Ben told me. I'll just be glad to be there and have a place to call home."

"So will I. We came all the way from Virginia. Where are you from?"

"Kansas. Things haven't been good there for a long time, and it seemed that this was our chance for a new start. Ben is a widower, and it had just become too hard for them all without his Ellie. I was widowed about a year ago and, well, I wanted to leave Kansas, too. This way I'll be able to help Ben with Matt and Hope, and we'll all be together."

The other woman nodded. "I can understand that. It's good when families are close. We never had any children, although we wanted to. Guess the good Lord figured we didn't need them. But if there's any way I can be of help, you just let me know."

"Thank you, Mrs. Lambert. You are making the run by yourself, then?"

"I am, but I've drove this team many a time. I'm not worried."

Faith decided right then that if this woman could make it on her own, she needn't worry about herself, Matt, and Hope. "Why don't you stay and have breakfast with us this morning?"

"Why thank you. I'll take you up on that invitation. I don't like eating alone."

Faith went to the wagon to get a skillet and some bacon just as Hope came out of the wagon, yawning.

"Good morning, dear. Did you sleep well?"

"I did. I had a dream I want to tell Papa about." Hope looked around the camp and back at Faith. "Where is he?"

Faith put an arm around her niece, knowing she wasn't going to like what she had to say. "He went on to the front of the line last night. He thinks he has a better chance of finding us a claim if he gets an early start."

Tears gathered in Hope's eyes, and she turned pale. "Why didn't he wake me before he left? How are we going to make it without him?"

"Why, first we'll pray, and then we'll trust the Lord to get us there. Hope dear, don't worry. Your papa will be there to meet us." She hugged her niece and then drew her over to meet Mrs. Lambert.

"Mrs. Lambert's husband left early, too, and she's going to go in on her own. If she can do it by herself, then we should be able to do it together. Don't you think?"

"Why. . .I suppose so. I'd just feel better if Papa was here."

Faith didn't say what she was feeling. . .that she wanted Ben there every bit as much as Hope did. Instead, she tried to reassure her niece and hoped she'd believe her. "Your papa wouldn't have left us if he wasn't sure that we could make it there without him."

At about that time, Faith noticed that Matt had wakened

and joined them. He was pulling his left suspender over his shoulder as he walked up to them with a grin. "Mornin'."

"Good morning, Matt. I'll have breakfast ready soon."

"I'm hungry as a bear," he said. "I can't wait to get started!"

"Aren't you upset that Papa isn't here, Matt?" Hope asked.

"Well, he talked to me about it," Matt said, sounding as if he'd helped make the decision. "He trusts me to get us there in one piece. We'll be all right."

His voice cracked a little at the end, but Faith didn't call attention to it. She could tell Matt was nervous, but he was trying hard to be a man about it all, and the least she could do was help him. "Sure we will be. With you driving and me coaching, we can't help but make it!" she teased.

"Matt is going to drive the team? But—"

"Your papa says he can do it. Matt says he can do it. And we're going to trust them."

"Oh, if I can do it, there's nothing to it," Mrs. Lambert put in, offering her two cents. "Your brother will be just fine, honey."

"Thank you, ma'am." Matt said, walking over to meet Mrs. Lambert. After Faith introduced them, he asked, "Are you going to drive yourself?"

"I am. And if I can do it, you can, too."

Faith got busy making breakfast as Matt and Mrs. Lambert talked about letting their teams lead unless they put them all in danger. Then they'd have to take over and slow them down.

Faith turned the bacon and thanked the Lord for sending Mrs. Lambert over to their campsite that morning. She glanced over her shoulder. Even Hope was chuckling at something the other woman had said.

# four

When the gunshot sounded at noon on April 22, Gabe was ready. Midnight wanted to go full speed, straining with all his might to keep up with the others, but Gabe held him to a slower pace, knowing he'd need more speed later on. He saw no need to tire out his mount at the beginning, as so many passing him by would be doing.

He caught a glimpse of Ben Thompson loping his horse along at about the same easy gait he was using and figured they were both of the same mind. They headed away from the river and out onto the prairie, and the smell of crushed grasses reminded Gabe of new mown hay. Long before the first hour was up, many of those mounts were already glistening with sweat in trying to keep up their pace. More than one horse and rider went down, and Gabe winced at the sound of a gunshot and then the acrid smell of gunpowder in the air as he passed a rider who'd had to put his mount out of his misery.

As he neared the town site of Guthrie, Gabe had to tamp down his natural urge to stop and help others as Midnight kicked up dust along the way. A few riders passed him, their horses' eyes rolling as their riders urged them on. He was more than a little proud when Midnight crossed the last creek without any problem and brought him to the other side.

He dared to look back to see several riders thrown when their mounts balked at entering the water, wanting to stop and drink, instead. He was glad to see Ben Thompson aside him. They exchanged a grin, gave their mounts a nudge, and made it a contest to see who got to Guthrie first, finally letting their horses run full out.

When they entered the town site, they had to slow down. People were milling around everywhere, and it was hard to tell just where they were. But as they headed down what they thought might be the main street and back up the next street over, Gabe knew he was going to choose the first unclaimed lot he could find—no matter where it might be.

It turned out to be not all that far from the train station and perhaps a little farther from the center of town than he might like—probably just on the edge of what would be the business center, but it would work for him. At this stage, it wouldn't pay to be picky.

Ben Thompson must have had the same idea because he reined his mount in to the lot next to the one Gabe unfurled his stake on. They had land. And both lots were pretty, with trees at the back. Gabe thought there might be a creek nearby. He hoped so anyway.

They took time to catch their breath and watched the goings on around them for a few minutes, and then Gabe pulled out his canvas-covered canteen and took a long swig. He didn't think he'd ever seen so many people milling around, laughing, arguing, and working to get a lean-to or tent up on a piece of land all at the same time. It looked like they were fortunate to have found the lots they did.

The city lots were supposed to be 25 feet wide and 140 feet deep, but it appeared some claims had been laid one right on top of another, and some had to be on streets. There'd be plenty of fights over those, that was for sure. Gabe checked his lot from one end to the other until he was satisfied that there was nothing there, no evidence that anyone else had tried to claim it. He noticed Ben doing the same thing before he began to set up a tent in one corner of his lot. Gabe got busy setting up his own. It was good to know the person on at least one side of his lot. They worked hard and finished at about the same time.

Ben came over to the lot line. "Glad to have you as a neighbor, Logan."

"Same here, Thompson. I'm glad we both got a lot. It was beginning to look doubtful that we'd find anything, and we were some of the first ones here. How do you think this many people got here before we did?"

Ben shook his head. "I don't know. My guess is some of them came in early on, and that's a shame when the rest of us had to wait."

"Well, from the looks of it, there'll be plenty of disputes. Maybe they'll get caught."

"Guess we'll see. Want to agree to watch out for each other's claim when one of us needs to be away?" Ben asked.

"I certainly do. It'll make keeping our claims a lot easier on us. Thanks for the offer."

"Thanks for accepting."

By midafternoon, they had met several others who'd staked claims nearby, and news rippled through the town site that the 320 acres set aside for the town of Guthrie was not near enough. Three other towns had grown out of what had started as one. The four towns were now Guthrie, East Guthrie, Capitol Hill, and West Guthrie.

"Reckon which town we're in?" Ben asked.

"I have no idea and don't much care at this point. I'm just glad to have a lot to lay claim to."

Ben grinned and nodded. Gabe figured he was going to

get along with his neighbor just fine.

"What time do you think your family will be getting in?" If Ben Thompson was going to be his neighbor, that meant his family would be there, too. Somehow that thought made Gabe feel good.

"I don't know. I'm hoping they'll be here before twilight. It'll be hard for Faith to spot me if it's after dark."

"I'm sure they'll be here before then," Gabe tried to assure his new friend. He hoped they'd make it in soon.

❧

The ride into Guthrie was much more harrowing than Faith had planned. She had to say that Matt did a wonderful job controlling their team. Right from the start, when the gunshot had rung out across the prairie, he'd done as Mrs. Lambert suggested and given the team their lead.

All appeared to be going just fine at first, but it was soon obvious that Matt would have to prove his mettle. They were in the middle of a stampede. All around them, wagons raced across the land—from large, covered ones like hers to open buckboards, runabouts, and carriages. Faith even saw a bicycle or two.

She and Hope held on for dear life as they watched one buggy hit a bog in the ground and turn over on its side. Faith's heart pounded in fear, but Matt managed to guide the team around it. He seemed to have everything under control, and Faith breathed a sigh of relief.

It was the roughest ride she'd ever had, and Faith hoped never to have another one like it. The wagon hit ruts and rocks, and they swayed back and forth over the grassy land. She prayed constantly that they wouldn't overturn, that they would get there without accident. And she prayed that Ben had gotten there safely and that Mrs. Lambert was all right.

They'd lost sight of her a ways back.

She was proud of Hope and Matt. Hope tried to hide her fear, but Faith could see it in her eyes. She gave her a quick hug and whispered, "Matt is handling this team as well as Ben does. He'll get us there safely. Don't worry."

Assuring her niece was one thing. Taking her own advice was quite another. She was worried, but it wasn't because of Matt. She didn't think she could have done as well as her young nephew. She might be older, but obviously he was more experienced with the team. Of course, he'd helped Ben in the fields and taken Hope into town when Ben was busy doing other things around the farm. Matt *was* growing up, and from here on out, she would take care to treat him like the young man he was becoming.

They crossed the creek coming off the Cimarron much easier than Faith had expected. Still, she held her breath until they were safely on the other side. Several wagons had more trouble, and at least one overturned into the cold water.

Her heart went out to those settlers, but she was thankful that none of them were Mrs. Lambert. It was getting late in the afternoon when they saw all of the white up ahead.

"What is that, Aunt Faith?" Hope asked. "It's not wagons like ours, is it?"

"Some of it might be. . .but I think those are tents. That must be Guthrie ahead!"

Matt flicked the reins and let the team go, yelling, "Yahoo! We're almost there!"

As they got closer, they could see that it was indeed a sea of tents. . .all over the prairie. As they reached the town site, Matt slowed the team down, and they followed a wagon ahead of them, hoping they'd find a way down the main street—if there was one.

Faith wasn't sure how they were going to find Ben, but she was going to trust that he would be on the lookout for them. Everything seemed to be in total confusion. Tents were everywhere, ranging from small ones to very large ones. She could see one already set up as a hotel from the sign outside, and then they passed a tent with a sign on it that read, RESTAURANT—OPEN SOON. Faith wondered if it was the Millers' place.

They continued down what she thought might be the main street, but she couldn't see Ben anywhere—and she wasn't sure he'd even be in the town. It could be that he'd tried to claim land out of town, but she hoped not.

"Do you think we took the wrong street, Aunt Faith?" Matt asked. "Should I turn around?"

"No, not yet. Besides, I'm not sure how you'd manage that in this crowd. Let's go on down until we find a place we can turn around. Surely we'll see Ben soon."

Hope's eyes were wide with excitement and fear at all she was seeing. "You don't think anything happened to Papa, do you, Aunt Faith?"

Faith's heart seemed to stop beating at the mere thought of anything happening to Ben. She shook off the very idea. No. The Lord wouldn't give them more than they could handle. She knew that. "I'm sure he's fine, Hope. We'll—"

"Faith! Hope!"

Faith looked around. She knew she'd heard Ben's voice.

"Over here! Matt!"

Matt turned his head this way and that. "I hear him. But I don't see him."

"There he is!" Hope pointed up ahead to where Ben was waving his hat and yelling at them.

Faith could feel her smile grow as she waved at her brother.

She'd never been so glad to see him in her entire life. From the look on his face, he was just as glad to see them.

Ben ran to meet them. "I was getting worried about you all. I can't tell you how glad I am to see you! I knew you could do it, Matt!"

Faith patted her nephew's shoulder. "He's every bit as good a driver as you are, Ben. Maybe better after today," she teased.

"Oh yeah?" He grinned and led them to the lot he'd claimed. He helped Faith and Hope down and hugged his daughter as she admonished, "You should have let me know you were goin' on ahead of us, Papa. Matt did real well, but I was worried about you, too!"

Ben hugged her again. "I'm sorry, Hope. I was afraid that you wouldn't sleep last night if we woke you up. But all is well. The Lord got us all here safely, and I think the first thing we need to do is thank Him."

Matt jumped down, and they formed a circle before Ben took off his hat and led them in prayer. "Dear Lord, we can't thank You enough for getting us all here today and for watchin' over us on the long trip here. We ask that You continue to guide our lives and help us to know what You want us to do in this new home of ours. We thank You most of all for Your plan for our salvation through Your precious Son and our Savior. It's in His name we pray Amen."

Ben put his hat back on and slapped Matt on the shoulder. "Let's unhitch the team and get them fed and watered, son. Faith, you and Hope just catch your breath; then we'll get settled in best we can for now."

Faith looked around at all the tents and people. "I've never seen anything like this, Hope."

"Me either, Aunt Faith." Hope shook her head as she took in all the sights and sounds.

Faith leaned against their wagon, glad to be standing instead of being jostled every which way, and looked and listened along with her niece. They could hear laughter and voices that rose in anger. Her heart gave a familiar twist at the faint cry of a baby in the distance, and along with it all was the constant sound of more people still coming in, hoping to find a piece of land to call their own, stirring up dust in the process.

"Aunt Faith, look! Isn't that the nice man who helped us when we got bogged down on the river?"

Faith glanced over in the direction Hope was pointing. On the next lot over, starting a campfire, stood a man who looked like the one who had helped them. The one who'd taken up residence in her daydreams ever since. She pulled Hope's arm down before the man saw her and said, "Don't point, dear. It's rude. But I think you are right. He certainly resembles the man."

He looked over just then, smiled, and tipped his hat to her and Hope.

Hope waved and Faith smiled. If he wasn't the man who had helped them, then he had to have an identical twin. . . and somehow she just didn't think that was the case.

# *five*

*Ben Thompson has a real nice family, no doubt about it*, Gabe thought as he watched them get settled in. They sure looked happy to be back together, too. Hard as he tried not to, Gabe felt envious. If only Laura had lived. . .no. He shook his head to ward off the thoughts. He couldn't let old memories of what might have been pull him down. There was no way to undo the past. He could only go forward. Maybe someday he'd have what Ben Thompson did, but for now, he'd just be thankful that he had his freedom and could start a new life.

Gabe busied himself getting what few belongings he'd brought with him into his tent and making a bed of sorts inside. Then he spread some of his things out over the lot so that no one could think he didn't have a claim on it. That's what he'd seen others do, and he hoped it worked. He and Ben had witnessed several fights taking place down the street, and he didn't want to have any trouble here.

He unpacked his saddlebags and looked over the meager provisions he had left. He should have stocked up on a few more things in Arkansas City. He had a couple of cans of beans, some jerky, hardtack, and coffee, but after smelling whatever it was that was cooking over on Ben's lot, none of what he had to choose from seemed very appetizing. He hoped the hunting was good around here.

He poured a cup of the coffee he'd made earlier and watched the activity around him. More tents were going up across the street—or what he assumed was going to be a street. From the looks of things, there would be more than enough business for anyone who knew how to use a hammer. That's what he knew, and what he planned on doing here if things worked out. He hadn't asked Ben Thompson what he was planning to do, but there'd be plenty of time to find out.

Gabe had been trying *not* to watch every move Ben's family made, but it was hard not to. It was beginning to look kind of homey over there. The woman and young girl had folded down their cook station at the side of the wagon and brought out some stools to sit on. Probably they'd straightened the inside of the covered wagon, too. Things were bound to have gotten topsy-turvy from the ride across the prairie.

Tired as they must be, they laughed as they went about their business, and just the sound of it lightened his mood. He couldn't keep from stealing a glance or two in their direction. Gabe took a drink of his lukewarm coffee and chided himself. He sure was getting nosy lately.

As the sun set and the sky turned to twilight, the twinkle of stars appeared, and campfires and lanterns lit up the night. Gabe figured he'd better pull out that hardtack. The aroma wafting over from Ben's lot was making his mouth water, and he didn't know when he'd been so hungry.

❧

While Ben and Matt saw to the stock, Faith started supper. She figured her brother and nephew had to be starving. They hadn't eaten since before the run, and Ben probably hadn't eaten since supper the night before.

She tried not to watch the handsome man on the other lot as she peeled potatoes, but it wasn't hard to see that he had few supplies with him. He couldn't carry that much on horseback—at least not like they could store on the wagon.

She was going to feel really awful to be eating supper when he had nothing but hardtack and beans.

She'd fried bacon earlier, and now she turned the potatoes she was frying in the grease. They were almost done, so she added some onions to them and moved them off the fire a bit. Then she set the leftover biscuits from supper the night before near the coals to warm them. It might not be much, but it was hot, and she was pretty sure it would be tasty.

When Ben and Matt came back from tending the stock, she wanted to ask her brother about the man on the lot to the right of them, but he brought up the subject before she had a chance to.

Ben took his hat off and washed his hands in some of the water Faith had in a tin dish just for that purpose. "You'll never guess who I made the run with. Remember that man who helped us get the wagon unstuck?"

*As if I could forget him.* "Of course I do." Her heart began to pound faster, catching up with, and keeping time to, the sound of the hoofbeats passing by their claim. "That man on the lot over there sure looks a lot like him."

"He's one and the same, and I'd kind of like to ask him to supper, if it's all right with you."

"Of course it is." So it was him. Faith's heart beat even faster. He'd been in her thoughts off and on ever since the day he helped them. "We're just having fried potatoes, bacon, and warmed-up biscuits, but it'll be a hot meal."

"I'm sure he'll appreciate it. I'll go get him." Ben marched over to the man, and Faith could hear him issue the invitation.

"Gabe, I'd like you to meet my family, and we'd all like to thank you for the help you gave us the other day. Faith is a mighty fine cook, and we have plenty. Won't you come take supper with us?"

She held her breath waiting for his answer. He didn't hesitate. "My stomach's been rumbling near an hour from the aroma coming from her fry pan. I'd be more than happy to accept your invitation."

Faith heard laughter and couldn't stop herself from glancing over to see Gabe coming back with Ben. "Get out one more plate, Hope. It appears that Mr. Logan is going to eat with us."

Her niece smiled. "I thought he might."

Faith turned the potatoes once more, trying not to watch as the two men walked over to the wagon. But when they reached her side, she stood straight and turned to meet their neighbor.

"Gabe Logan, this is my family," Ben said.

*Finally,* Faith thought. A name to put to the face she'd been unable to get out of her mind.

"This is my sister, Faith Anderson; my daughter, Hope; and my son, Matt, who got them all here safely," Ben introduced them. "Both Faith and I are widowed, and it seemed a good idea to make a new start here. I really appreciate her coming out here with us to be here for my children.

Gabe held out a hand to each one, ending with Faith. She wiped her hands on her apron and held out her hand. "I'm pleased to meet you, Mr. Logan."

Gabe Logan took his hat off, smiled as he enveloped her hand in his larger one, and looked down into her eyes. "I'm pleased to meet you all, and I'm glad you got here safe and sound. I've been trying to keep your brother from worrying overly much, but if you hadn't shown up soon, I think he'd have been out looking for you."

Surprised at the shock of electricity that shot up her arm

when Gabe Logan took her hand, Faith quickly slipped her hand from his. "I'm glad he had someone to talk to while he waited." She sounded a little breathless to her own ears and took a calming breath. "Supper will be ready in a few minutes."

"I've smelled it ever since you started frying that bacon. I can tell you I'll be glad to wait as long as it takes to have a taste of your cookin', ma'am."

Faith was glad it was getting dark. She felt the color flood her face at his compliment. She could only hope her cooking tasted as good as he thought it smelled.

Ben showed him where to wash up while she and Hope dished up their supper. Ben brought out a bench from the wagon, and with the stools they already had out, everyone had a place to sit. Once they'd all taken a plate and settled down, Ben said the blessing.

It was a relief to have them all together, and it felt nice to have company. Supper tasted pretty good to Faith, but with the way Gabe went on about it, she wondered how long it had been since he had any home cooking. Where was his family? She was a bit surprised when she heard herself voice her next thought aloud: "Will your wife be joining you soon, Mr. Logan?"

He swallowed the bite he'd been chewing and shook his head. "No, ma'am. I'm not married. It's just me out here."

"Oh. I'm sorry, Mr. Logan. I had no business asking." Faith felt terrible. Just because she wanted to know if he was married—and she knew that was why she'd asked—she had no right to bring him sorrow, and something in his voice that told her she had.

"Nothin' wrong with asking a body about himself, I reckon."

"So what are you planning on doing here, Gabe?" Ben

asked, changing the subject, much to Faith's relief.

"I'm a builder by trade. From the looks of the growing population, I think this town might be able to support as many as come here. What about y'all? What are you going to do?"

Ben laughed, and Faith listened to his answer closely. "Beats me. I intended on getting a section to farm or ranch, but when we got here, I was afraid to pass up an unclaimed lot. I knew the family would be looking for me, and I didn't want them to have to wander around out on the prairie. I think Faith wanted a place in town, anyway. Coming here seemed a good way to make a new start for both of us. Guess we have some decisions to make, but there's time. I'm just glad we have a claim. Once it's official, we can figure out what to do next."

Faith breathed a sigh of relief. She did want to live in town, and she thought Matt and Hope would be better off there. Ben was such a good big brother, thinking of what she might want, but she did want him to be happy, too. She hoped they could come up with a way to see that they all were.

The rest of the meal passed pleasantly, with Matt and even Hope getting in on the conversation and all of them telling about their rides into Guthrie.

Faith brought out a peach cobbler she'd made the day before and put near the fire to warm while they ate supper. She sure was glad she'd used the last of the peaches they'd brought with them when she saw the way Gabe Logan's eyes brightened as she cut into it.

He took the plate she handed him and sighed. "I think I'll just savor the smell for a minute. I can't even remember the last time I enjoyed cobbler, ma'am. Thank you."

"You haven't even tasted it yet. It might not be to your liking."

"I tasted your fried potatoes and onions and your biscuits. Anyone who can cook that good—well, Mrs. Anderson, there's not a doubt in my mind how this cobbler's going to taste."

Faith loved to cook, and her family had always been appreciative of her meals, but she'd never felt quite so complimented as she did tonight. She poured coffee to go with the cobbler and felt good that she'd managed to feed this man who had no one to cook for him.

After supper, while she and Hope cleaned up, Ben and Gabe went out and met some of the neighbors. It wasn't long before Ben brought a man and his wife, a woman about Faith's age, to meet her.

"Faith, this is Mr. and Mrs. Littleton. They've come all the way from New York. Mr. Littleton works for the railroad. I thought it'd be nice if you and Mrs. Littleton met."

"I'm pleased to meet you, Mrs. Littleton." It was impossible not to notice that she was expecting a baby, and soon from the looks of it. Faith tried to tamp down the ever-present sorrow she felt at never having had a child of her own.

"Oh, please call me Amy. I'm so glad to meet you," Mrs. Littleton said. "I've never been away from home before now, and I was wondering if there might be another woman close by. Then I saw you setting up camp this afternoon, and I was so relieved."

"Well, there may not be many of us here yet, but once some of these men get settled, I'm sure they'll be bringing in their families," Faith said. She had a feeling the young woman needed some assurance. "If you don't mind my asking, when is your baby due?"

Amy laughed. "I thought for sure it would come today, but it's not due for another few weeks. I'm hoping to find a doctor in the area by then."

"Surely you will. Would you like a piece of cobbler? I have some left from supper."

"Oh, no, thank you. I ate not long ago. I just wanted to meet you. I'll sleep better tonight knowing there is another woman nearby. I'd like to sit though, if it's all right?"

"Oh yes. Please take a seat." Faith felt bad for not offering her a place to sit sooner. The woman looked exhausted. "Would you like some tea? It won't take long to make some."

Amy shook her head as she eased down onto one of the stools. "No, that's all right, but thank you. It's nice just to have some female company. My mother will be glad to know I've met someone when she gets my next letter. She hated to see us leave."

"New York is quite far away." Faith wanted to ask why they had come so far from their family, but she'd asked enough nosy questions for one night and decided to talk about the future instead. "I have a feeling that Guthrie will be a nice-sized town very soon. I never dreamed there would be this many people settling here."

"No, neither did I. It is going to be exciting to see it grow from a prairie full of tents to a real town." Amy smiled. "My husband, John, says there are going to be some real clashes over some of these lots. We saw two fistfights just today!"

"Oh dear, I'm glad I missed that."

"It wasn't very pleasant." Amy shivered.

They talked about all kinds of things from babies—Amy wanted a girl, and her husband wanted a boy—to setting up housekeeping in a wagon or tent, until her husband said they should be going.

Faith watched Mr. Littleton help his wife across the street. She thought she was as happy as Amy to know another woman nearby.

Gabe decided he needed to leave, too. "I don't want to wear out my welcome. I thank you folks for letting me share your supper. It was mighty good, Mrs. Anderson."

"You're welcome and thank you. But please call me Faith."

"Only if you'll call me Gabe.

Faith nodded. "Then thank you, Gabe."

"You're welcome. . .Faith." He told Matt and Hope goodnight and then tipped his hat to Faith. "Goodnight."

"Goodnight."

Ben walked back over to Gabe's lot with him, and Faith and Hope went inside the wagon and got ready for bed. She didn't think she'd have any problem sleeping tonight. After staying awake half the night before and making the run today, she should sleep very well. It helped that she'd met some neighbors, too. With Ben and Matt sleeping in the tent nearby and Gabe Logan across the way, Faith felt safe in a sea of strangers. She said her nightly prayers, yawned, and closed her eyes.

❧

Gabe went back to his claim with a full stomach and a lighter heart. He and Ben had agreed to watch over each other's claims when one or the other had to go somewhere. He liked the man and his family, and he'd really enjoyed their company tonight.

The night had promised to be long and lonesome before Ben had come to ask him to supper. It had turned out to be a wonderful start in this new town.

Ben's sister looked exhausted from the run, and he didn't know how she'd been able to do that, get settled in, and be willing to have company for supper. She'd been so welcoming and nice to him and to the Littletons when they'd come over. He was impressed with her sweet disposition.

Gabe poured the last dregs of his coffee. It didn't compare to Faith's. Supper had indeed been as good as it had smelled. It'd been a long time since he'd had a meal like that. He'd never had cobbler any better, and those fried potatoes and onions were cooked just right. The potatoes had been crisp and tender, and he was still wondering why the onions hadn't burned.

He poured his bad coffee on the fire, lit a lantern, and went into his tent. He was tired but content. He'd claimed a nice lot in what appeared to be the edge of town, he had good neighbors, and he was looking forward to the future instead of back to the past.

He lay down on the bed he'd put together and folded his hands behind his head. If he was honest with himself, he had to admit that he was glad to know that Faith was Ben's sister and not his wife. Possibly it was because he'd been thinking about her and that fiery hair ever since the day he'd helped them at the river.

Figuring she was married to Ben the first time he'd seen them, he'd been quite irritated with himself for thinking about her at all. But even after Ben introduced her as his sister, Gabe's eye had been drawn to the ring on her finger. He sure was glad Ben had explained about her being a widow.

He hadn't given any thought to another woman since Laura died, and he wasn't sure why Ben's sister had taken up so many of his thoughts in the last few days. He hadn't even known her then. He had a feeling it wasn't going to be easy to put her out of his mind now that he knew who she was and that she wasn't Ben's wife—especially now that he knew she wasn't waiting for a husband to join her. Still, he had to do it. He had a past he didn't want to share and a sorrow he wasn't over. He had no business thinking about the pretty redhead across the way—no business at all.

# six

Ben was watching Gabe's lot while Gabe went to file his claim, and Faith had just poured a cup of coffee to take over to him, when a stranger strode over and began yelling at her brother.

"What do you think you're doing? Stealin' my claim?" The man looked mad and mean, and Faith didn't know whether to walk slowly so as not to spill the coffee or throw it down and run to her brother's defense.

"Look, mister, who are you and what are you talking about?" Ben motioned for Faith to stay where she was as he approached the man. "I'm not stealing anyone's claim."

"Name's Frank Jarvis, and I'm sayin' this is my lot an' you stole it right out from under me."

"I don't know what you are talking about, Jarvis," Ben said. "There was nothin' on this claim when I got here. No stake, not you, nor any of your things. I checked real good from one corner to the other."

"You're a lyin'."

"My pa isn't a liar," Matt had come from the back of the lot to join Ben, his fists clenched at his side.

"Well, I say he is." The man named Jarvis spat a cud of tobacco on the ground.

Matt took a step forward, and the breath caught in Faith's throat as Ben held him back.

"Mister, you'd better get off this lot now."

Gabe seemed to appear from nowhere, and Faith let out a relieved sigh that Ben would have someone besides her and

43

the kids on his side. Hope had joined her at the campfire, and Faith had to grab her arm to keep her from running to her father's side.

"Mr. Thompson isn't lying," Gabe said.

"Jest who are you?" Jarvis asked.

"Name is Gabe Logan. What's it to you?"

"Seems like I've seen you before. Where you come from?"

"Don't think that's any of your business. If we'd ever have met, I'd a remembered it."

"You sure?"

"I'm positive. But back to your accusation—Ben isn't lying. He and I came in together. We both staked our claims at the same time and made sure no one else had laid claim to either of them."

"Then you must be a liar, too, Logan. I put claim to this lot over here right off."

"Right off when?" Ben asked. "Did you come in early? You weren't anywhere to be seen when I got here."

Several other men gathered around. "I was here before these men came in," said an older man Faith had seen the day before. "I never saw you though. I think you must be mixed up about your claim."

"You stay out of it. This is between me and this man, mister." Jarvis nodded toward Ben.

"Well if it is between us, Jarvis, I repeat, no claim was on this lot when I got here," Ben said. "And if you had laid claim to it, why didn't you say so last night?"

"I didn't want to disturb your womenfolk. They looked like they was tired out."

"Well that's right nice of you, but this isn't your claim, and I'm not handin' it over to you," Ben began to advance toward Jarvis, and Gabe fell into step beside him.

"Well, maybe not right now." Jarvis began to back up as the two men walked toward him. "But you will. I'll be gitt'n this lot. You can be assured of that fact. I'll see you in court."

"Don't count on it, Jarvis. Now get off my lot, and don't come back."

"Oh, I'm goin' for now." He turned to leave and then looked back at Gabe. "I've seen you before. I know I have."

"Well I've never seen you till today."

"I've seen you, an I'll remember sooner or later." He turned back to Ben. "I'll be back ta claim what's mine. You can count on it."

When Ben reached out to grab him by the collar, Jarvis turned and saw that more men had gathered around. "You'll all see. I'll be back, and this claim'll be mine!"

He hightailed it off the lot, and Faith breathed a sigh of relief. But a shiver of fear shot down her spine. The man meant to get this lot. She was sure of it.

❧

As soon as Jarvis was out of sight, Gabe asked, "Where'd that man come from? Is he crazy or what?"

"I don't know," Ben shook his head. "He may think he's seen you, but I really do have a feeling I've seen him somewhere before. I just can't remember where it was."

"I think I saw him watching us yesterday, Ben," Faith said. "You probably did, too."

Gabe was glad to see some of the color back in her face. She'd looked pale as a ghost when he'd got back to the claim. If nothing else, that the stranger had frightened her made the man one Gabe would keep his eye on from now on.

"Why don't you two go on and file that claim now—before Jarvis decides to cause more trouble? I'll stay here and make sure he doesn't come back."

Gabe intended to stand by Ben, his sister, and his children no matter what Jarvis tried to stir up. He wasn't going to let some bully take their claim. He couldn't help but wonder how many false accusations about stealing claims would be levied in the coming weeks.

"Thanks, Gabe. But there's also that general assembly I've heard about set for later this afternoon. They want everyone there to get a government put together. What are we goin' to do about that?"

"You and Gabe can go. Matt and I will watch the claims."

"I don't know if I can leave you here by yourselves, Faith."

"Ben, you and Gabe aren't going to be able to keep watch every minute. There is too much to do to get settled here. We'll be all right."

With that kind of commotion going on, Gabe decided that maybe it was time to visit the U.S. marshal's office and make sure no one could make trouble for him. He didn't want the problems in his past to cause him trouble now. And he sure didn't want anything to keep him from trying to help Ben and his family. He'd do that after Ben and Faith got back from filing their claim. No sense in leaving things to chance.

❧

Faith was still unsettled as she and Ben headed toward the land office to file their claim. There was no truth to Frank Jarvis's claim. She knew that. Still, he meant to take it from them if he could. Had he already made a claim?

When she voiced her concern to Ben, he tried to shrug it off, but she knew him well—and he was just as troubled by the man's accusations as she was.

"I don't see how he could as he's not on the land. But I'm sure he'll try later on. For now, we're going to make it legal and then pray the man doesn't cause a ruckus, or that if he tries to, he won't succeed. That's really all we can do, Faith."

She knew he was right, and she tried to put the worry behind her. The Lord would take care of them; that she knew. He always had. And she was glad that they had Gabe Logan as their neighbor. The way he had come to Ben's defense had made her already good opinion of him raise another notch.

Her brother voiced almost the same thing. "I'm glad to have Gabe on the lot next to ours. I wouldn't have left Hope and Matt there after Jarvis's visit if Gabe weren't there."

"And I wouldn't want you to. But they'll be fine there with me, too."

"I don't know, sis—"

"Ben, I'm a grown woman." Faith stopped in the middle of the road and turned to her brother, both hands on her hips. "I can scream with the best of them. Besides, our neighbors have seen us. They know we've been there. I don't think Frank Jarvis will try anything else today, anyway. He's bound to be at that assembly, too."

"And if he sees me and Gabe, he might try to take over while we're gone."

"Ben, Matt has a shotgun, and I know you've taught him how to use it. And I—"

"I know. You're right. We can't stay there twenty-four hours a day. But we do need to be on the lookout for Jarvis all the time. I know the Lord knows the truth, but I do feel like that man is going to try to cause some trouble. If not today or tomorrow, eventually. You do remember how to use a gun, don't you?"

"Why of course. Papa taught us both at the same time. And you kept saying a girl didn't need to know how."

"Well I was wrong, and I'm glad Papa taught you. I'll leave my shotgun with you."

"No need. I have Noah's derringer. And I'll use it if I have to. But I hope it never comes to that."

"So do I, Faith. So do I."

They'd reached the land office by then, and though the line was long, it seemed to be moving fairly fast.

As they inched forward, Faith turned to her brother. "I probably should have stayed behind to watch Matt and Hope. You really don't need me to file claim to the lot."

"Yes, you do need to be here. I'm not claiming the lot for me."

"What?"

"We're going to put it in your name. You're the one who wants to live in town, Faith. And I'm going to see you settled in good. But I'd still like to find some land outside of town for a farm or small ranch."

"But what about the children, Ben? Don't you think it would be best for them to stay in town?"

"Possibly. And they will be for a while, Faith. No need to make a bunch of decisions right now. There's plenty of time for that. I just want the lot in your name. Even more so after our visit from Jarvis. And I want to make sure you get settled in. You need to be thinking on what you might want to do with it."

Faith knew she wanted to be able to provide for herself, and she had several ideas about how to do it. That her brother was helping her accomplish this brought tears to her eyes.

She gave him a hug, even though she was sure it embarrassed him. "Oh Ben. Thank you! I don't know what to say. Are you sure?"

"I'm positive. Just figure out what you want to do. We'll get you settled in, and then I'll find my own place."

Faith nodded and sighed. "I wish you'd stay in town, too, but I don't want you to be unhappy, Ben." He deserved to have what he wanted. "Do you think you'll be able to find something that isn't too far out?"

"I'll try to, sis. Maybe by the time I get to looking, some of these people will decide to go back home."

"You don't think they'll stay?"

"Some will. Some won't. They either won't be able to make a go of it, or they won't want to. They'll miss what they had."

"We'll stay."

"Yes, we will."

It took several hours, but finally they had the papers in hand and started back to the claim. Faith felt the pride of ownership for the first time. When they got back, she was relieved to find things peaceful and to know that Jarvis hadn't come back to bother them.

"Everything has been calm over here," Gabe said. "But there've been a couple of other rifts over claims on down the street."

"Gabe and I made some traps and put them at the back of our lots, Pa. We've already caught a couple of rabbits!" Matt said.

"Oh, that is wonderful news, Matt. I was wondering what we'd have for supper tonight." Faith didn't wait for her brother to issue an invitation for Gabe to join them. "You'll take supper with us again, won't you? It's the least we can do for you watching the claim while we were gone."

"I'd be crazy to turn down an invitation to supper with you, Faith. Thank you." He turned to Gabe. "Are we both going to the assembly?"

Faith nodded at Ben. "You both should go. We'll be all right. Matt is here and—"

"I'll watch over Aunt Faith and Hope, Pa." Matt stood straight and tall. "You trusted me to get them here safely. I can protect them."

Matt had his Pa between a rock and a hard place, and Faith could tell Ben knew it. He'd been trying to teach Matt to be a man. He couldn't deny him the chance to be one now.

Ben let out a sigh and nodded. "All right. This meeting shouldn't take that long. I'll be back soon."

"I do need to run an errand after the meeting," Gabe said. "What time should I be back for supper?"

"Oh, don't worry. I'll wait to start supper until Ben comes back. It'll be ready about an hour or so after that. Will that give you enough time?"

"That should give me plenty of time." He turned to Ben. "You'll watch my claim?"

"You don't need to ask."

Gabe nodded and grinned before turning to Faith and tipping his hat. "I'll see you all after while, then."

Faith watched them leave, but it was Gabe her mind was on, wondering what it was about his smile that made her catch her breath. Perhaps it was because it was so rare. When they first met, he had the saddest eyes she'd ever seen, but every once in a while now his eyes sparkled, and she waited for those moments, was beginning to realize that they happened a little more often as he spent time with her and Ben and his children.

Perhaps he had no family. He'd never talked about his past, and she couldn't help but wonder what had put such sadness in his soul that it reached into his eyes.

❧

Gabe came away from the marshal's office, feeling as if he could finally start that new life here. Even if Frank Jarvis tried to make trouble for him somehow, the marshal knew the truth. He felt as if a load had been lifted off his shoulders, and he was looking forward to the future. When he got back to his claim, he hurried down to the creek to clean up a bit. Faith Anderson was a lady, and he wasn't going to come to her table without sprucing up.

The mouth-watering aroma of Faith's cooking drifted over from the next lot. His stomach gave an appreciative rumble as he made his way over to his neighbors'.

"Good evening, Gabe. Did you get your errands done?" Ben came around the wagon just as Gabe reached the campfire.

"I did. Did you fill your family in on the happenings at the assembly?"

"I did. It's too bad we couldn't come up with a mayor-elect today and that things got so agitated that the Camp Guthrie troops had to be called in. At least we have them until a city government can be formed."

"It'll just take a few days to get a good count for the mayor. We'll go cast our votes tomorrow and hope it's settled then."

"A lot of men want to run things, that's for sure. Let's hope we elect the right ones."

"Yep. Once we get a government in place, I think Guthrie is going to grow to be a fine city," Gabe said.

Faith lifted the lid to the pot hanging over the fire and began to stir the contents. "It's about ready. I hope you all are hungry."

"Mmm. Smells wonderful." Gabe hoped he spoke loud enough to cover his growling stomach.

"Thank you," Faith said as she turned from the pot. "I hope it's good. We're running low on vegetables."

"I heard that a train is bringing in supplies tomorrow.

Several big tents have Mercantile signs on them. Maybe they'll have some grocery supplies in a few days."

"Oh, I hope so. This took most of the potatoes and the last of the carrots. But there should be enough to feed the five of us until supplies start coming in."

Gabe felt warm inside as he realized she'd included him in her count. "Well, if you are going to keep inviting me to supper, I'm going to have to chip in for supplies."

"We won't be talking about that for a while," Ben said. "To our way of thinking, we owe you for all the help you've given us."

"I think this meal will cover whatever it is you think you owe me."

"Well then, there is just the opportunity to be neighborly," Faith added as she began ladling up the stew. She added a slice of cornbread from an iron skillet sitting near the fire and handed each of them their plate. Then she fixed her own and joined them on one of the seats around the fire.

After Ben said the blessing, Gabe took a bite and closed his eyes. It was every bit as good as it smelled. Faith was some cook. He opened his eyes to find her gaze on him, but she quickly turned away, and he wondered what she was thinking.

"This is wonderful, Faith. It's been a long time since I've had good cooking. I've learned to make a decent pot of coffee, but my cooking skills aren't very good. I manage to burn most of what I cook—and what isn't burnt is usually a little raw. I just never have managed to get the hang of it."

"Thank you, Gabe." Faith's face colored pink from the compliment, and he thought how pretty she was.

"Don't feel bad, Gabe," Ben said. "I'm a terrible cook, too. Even the kids can cook better'n me. I'm hoping Faith will give Matt some pointers. A man ought to know how to cook for himself, if nobody else. Having Faith around is a real blessing in more ways than one."

Gabe wasn't about to argue with his new friend there. He thought it was a blessing that his lot was right next to theirs and that he'd been invited to eat, maybe even on a regular basis. When Faith brought out a fresh berry pie, he sighed and sent up a silent prayer, thanking the Lord above for his new friends.

"Have you given any more thought to what you are going to do?" he asked Ben.

"With the claim?"

"Yep."

"Well, that's kind of up to Faith. We put the lot in her name. I'd still like to find me a place to farm or raise some cattle—but I won't do it until I get Faith settled here in town. By then, I'm hoping I'll get a good deal from someone who wants to be bought out."

"That's a possibility. I know I won't be one of those going back."

"Neither will we. We came to stay. In a few months, this place will be well on its way to being a regular town with all we need, but there'll be some hardships along the way. We're prepared for it."

"We are," Faith agreed. "If Matt can keep catching rabbits and the berry bushes hold out for a while. I still have staples and canned goods left. We should be okay until some of the merchants begin getting supplies."

Ben nodded. "Besides, neither of us have anything in Kansas to go back to."

It seemed to Gabe that they were of the same mind. They'd both had heartaches, just as he had. Somehow it comforted him to realize that.

## seven

Later that night after Gabe had gone back to his lot, the dishes had been washed, and Matt and Hope had settled down for the night, Ben and Faith enjoyed a last cup of coffee and watched the dying embers of the campfire.

"Now we have made claim on the lot, we can get on with settling in here. Have you had time to think about what you might want to do, Faith?"

She took a sip of coffee and nodded. "I think I'd like to open a boardinghouse. I've been trying to come up with something that would provide a living and a home, and the more I think about it, the better it sounds."

Her brother grinned over at her. "That's a good idea. From the looks of it, the town lots are all taken. There will be people coming in to work in the businesses that are about to be started up. They'll need a place to live. You are a right smart woman, little sister."

"Thank you, Ben. I think it will work. Best of all, I'll have a home of my own and a way to make a living to keep it."

"I'd like to think you'd marry again one day, sis."

"I've never said I wouldn't marry again." For some reason, Gabe Logan came to mind, and she looked over at his lot to see a glimmer of light shining from under his tent. If Ben noticed she looked that way, he didn't say anything, and for that she was thankful. She'd been thinking about their neighbor entirely too much the last few days. She was going to have to stop that. No man wanted a woman who couldn't have children, but she didn't want to go into all of that with her brother right now.

"You are much too young to live the rest of your life alone."

"It's just not something I'm looking to do right now. And if I ever do, I'll still have something in my name. Thank you for that, Ben. My in-laws didn't seem to care if I had a way to make a living or not. I'm thankful that Noah provided a way to get away from them and grateful to you for putting the claim in my name. Now I don't have to feel I must marry."

"You'd never have to do that, Faith. You'd always have a home with me if you needed it."

"I know that, Ben. But I'd like to see you marry again one day, too, you know. Matt and Hope are growing up, and they'll have their own lives one day. You don't want to live the rest of your life alone, Ben. Molly wouldn't want that either."

Her brother was silent for a while, and she felt bad for bringing his Molly to mind. "I'm sorry, Ben. I didn't mean to bring sad memories to you."

"Those memories are always with me, Faith. You certainly didn't cause them. My children do miss their mother— almost as much as I do—but I am so glad they have an aunt who loves them. I can't say what the future will bring to either of us in the way of finding others to love, but I can tell you that knowing you are here for Matt and Hope, should anything happen to me, gives me a comfort I treasure. Thank you for coming with us."

"Thank you for asking me to join you. I'm just as thankful I have you three in my life."

As they finished their coffee in silence, Faith glanced over at Gabe's once more. It saddened her that he had no one. She might not have a husband or children of her own, but how blessed she was that she had Ben and his children to share her life with.

Rolling thunder broke into her thoughts, and the smell of rain had her and Ben jumping to their feet. Faith emptied the coffee pot and grabbed their cups as a cooling wind swept in, and Ben hurried to cover the embers before they could begin to fly.

Ben made sure she was in the wagon and the flap was tied securely. " 'Night, sis. Stay dry," he yelled as he hurried to the tent to join Matt.

Faith quickly got ready for bed and slipped between the covers, glad that Hope slept peacefully while rain began to pour. She hoped Gabe was all settled in his tent. Her heart went out to him. How lonesome he must be over there, all alone with a storm coming and no one to share his life with.

❧

Afraid his neighbors would think he was taking advantage of their hospitality, Gabe had made himself say goodnight and go back to his tent and turn in. He could have stayed with Ben and his family for another hour or so, but he didn't want to wear out his welcome.

He'd enjoyed their company the last two evenings more than was good for him. He could get used to sharing meals with them, get used to seeing Faith's sweet face each day much too easily. He didn't know if claiming a lot next to them was a good thing or not. But the fact was they were neighbors and—a gust of wind hit the side of his tent, and the smell of rain came with it.

The temperature took a sudden drop, and Gabe shivered. He looked outside to see a solid sheet of rain. He could barely see a light from the tent and wagon over on Ben's—no Faith's—lot. From the looks of things, they'd turned in before the storm hit and should be safe and dry. He hoped so. He tied down the tent flap as well as he could and dove into his bedroll, pulling up every cover he had against the chill.

He was still cold the next morning, but he was glad to see the sun shining. Mud holes were everywhere, but his tent had stayed dry inside, and he was glad of that. He'd just started to put a pot of coffee on when Ben yelled over at him, "Faith has breakfast about ready. Come on over."

Gabe didn't have to be asked twice as he strode over to grab the cup of hot coffee Faith held out to him. Even after she fixed everyone a plate of bacon, biscuits, and gravy, she had plenty left over.

"Looks like you were cooking for an army this morning, Faith," Ben said.

"After last night, I thought I'd better have some cooking done in case another gully-washer comes or the wind picks up again and I can't get out to cook." She looked at Gabe and smiled. "I'll send a few biscuits and some bacon back with you, in case it storms again and you don't want to get out."

"I'd sure appreciate that, Faith. But I sure hope that doesn't happen."

"Me either," Matt said. "That tent held up real well, but I don't want to be stuck there for days."

"Being in the wagon with it swaying in the wind wasn't the greatest either," Hope added.

"But we all made it fine, and we'll be all right if it happens again," Faith said. "We'd better thank the good Lord for that. Some of these people are in lean-tos, or were yesterday. I wonder how they fared."

Wanting to reassure her, Gabe said, "We can check out the town after breakfast. Have you seen any sign of Frank Jarvis this morning?"

"No. Maybe that storm scared him off. I hope so." Ben took a bite of biscuit and gravy, and Gabe did the same.

Gabe thought he'd gone back to his childhood. No one could make gravy like his mother—except for Faith Anderson. "This is wonderful, Faith. I haven't tasted gravy this good since I was a kid."

"I'm sure you're exaggerating a bit, Gabe, but thank you."

Her cheeks turned that pretty shade of pink again, and Gabe's heart warmed when she smiled. "No, I'm not. You are an excellent cook."

"I guess we'd better get to that assembly 'fore long," Ben said. "Maybe we'll have a mayor by the end of the day." He looked over at his sister. "Are you sure you, Matt, and Hope will be all right here alone, Faith?"

"We'll be fine," Faith patted the pocket of her apron. "I have my gun, and Matt hasn't let his shotgun out of his sight since he woke up this morning."

Gabe took a last bite of his breakfast and a swig of coffee. "I'm ready when you are. If it goes on too long, one of us can come back and check in on things."

"That's a good plan, Gabe," Ben said. "Matt, you take care of things while we're gone."

"Yes, sir."

As they left the claim and headed toward the land office near where the assembly was held, Gabe wasn't sure who was most nervous about leaving Faith and Hope there with Matt. . .Ben or him.

❧

Trying to keep busy, Faith baked a pie from the berries she had left from the day before, and then she checked the supplies she had on hand. She was glad that they'd stocked up at Arkansas City. She was low on fresh vegetables, but she had some canned goods and plenty of flour and sugar.

Tonight, all she'd have to do was heat up the leftover stew. But she liked to be prepared, and she worried that if the weather kept Gabe from joining them, he'd go hungry. She wrapped up some biscuits and leftover bacon to send back with him that evening.

Matt kept watch on both claims, and Faith tried not to let on that she was keeping watch over him. Although she prayed she'd never have to use the gun in her pocket, she felt a certain amount of calm knowing it was there. Even though she wasn't prepared to admit it to them, she was glad when Ben and Gabe got back.

"Well, do we have a mayor?"

"Not yet. The two that were in the running yesterday, Hill and Hoogatt, were finally asked to withdraw, but they refused. The Camp Guthrie Troops had to be called in," Ben said.

"And still no mayor?"

Gabe chuckled and shook his head. "Not yet. But there is hope that we will have one soon. Cooler heads prevailed, and it was decided they would select three men from each faction, let them choose another man, and then choose the mayor. We're not sure why we even showed up. The crowd was so large it was hard to hear half of what was going on, and only a few really had any say at all."

"Yeah. Seems there are those who think they are the only ones qualified to run the town. And it isn't us," Ben laughed. "Just pray we get someone who's honest and wants the best for the people who came to settle here."

As Faith began getting their supper ready, they talked about what was going on around them.

"Several hotels and restaurants have opened up. All in

tents, but talk is that lumber is coming in daily and will keep coming long as it's needed," Gabe said.

"Several came in here with wagons of lumber and have already got started building their homes or places of business. In a few weeks, there will be real buildings up." Ben took the cup of coffee his sister handed him.

"I wonder how long it will take to build a boardinghouse," Faith said, pouring a cup for Gabe.

"I've been talkin' to Gabe about that," Ben said. "I forgot to tell you that he's a builder by trade, and well, we've agreed to help each other so that we can get his business and yours up and running."

Faith whirled around, spoon in hand. "Really?"

"Really. And we're going to start with the boardinghouse."

Faith put a hand over her pounding heart. Her newfound dream really was going to become a reality. She hugged her brother, and only proper etiquette kept her from hugging Gabe Logan, too. "Oh, thank you. Gabe, you'll have a room at the boardinghouse as long as you need it."

"You're welcome. But it looks like I'm getting the best end of the deal," Gabe said. "I get help building my office and a roof over my head and your good cooking while I build it."

"I don't know that's fair payment for seeing a dream come true. I just thank the Lord that we met up with you on the way and that you and Ben crossed paths again. We'll always be beholden to you, Gabe Logan."

He shook his head. "We're just helping each other, is all."

"We need to get a surveyor out to make sure we aren't going to have to move our property lines and then get some plans drawn up for your house, Faith."

Her house. Faith blinked against the sudden tears that threatened. She'd never had a home of her own. The house she and her husband had lived in belonged to his family, and she'd felt she had to check with his mother about anything she might want to change. After Noah passed away, her in-laws made it no secret that they wanted her gone. She hadn't been able to provide them with a grandchild, and with their son dead, they had no need for her in their lives. They'd never thought she was good enough for Noah, and only the fear of their peers finding out that they'd turned their daughter-in-law out on the streets kept them from doing just that. Now she would have a place no one could take from her and a way to make her own living from it.

"How many stories are you thinking?" Gabe asked. "If you're going to have boarders, you'll need more bedrooms. I can draw you up a few plans, if you'd like. Then you can see which one meets your needs the best."

"That sounds wonderful, Gabe. What size it is will of course depend on the price of building it. My late husband did leave me enough to get a good start here, I believe, but I—"

"Faith, there won't be a cost on my end—only the price of the materials and furnishings for you. You'll be furnishing me a home until I can build my own, not to mention the free advertising I'll get from people seeing it being built."

"Oh, I can't—"

"Yes, ma'am, you can. After all, Ben and Matt will be doing as much work as I will be. More like twice as much."

Put that way, it didn't sound quite so much like charity. And even if it was, she thanked the Lord for bringing this man into their lives. She hoped they could be as much of a blessing to him as he was to them.

"Do we have an agreement?" Gabe asked.

"We'd be crazy to say no. Wouldn't we, Faith?" Ben held

out his hand. He and Gabe shook hands, and then Gabe turned to her. "Faith?"

She nodded, held out her hand, and smiled. "We have a deal."

❧

Gabe was glad Faith had insisted on sending biscuits, bacon, and a slice of pie back with him that night, because for the next several days the wind blew so hard the only thing they could do was tie down the best they could and pray it ended soon. He wished he and Ben had been able to put up a more secure structure before the weather hit. He couldn't keep out the dust. It covered everything. After the wind and dust, the rains came again, and now mud was everywhere. Gabe thought it would never stop.

He was thankful he'd tucked a tablet and pens in his saddlebag. At least he'd been able to work on Faith's house plans. They were coming along nicely, and he thought she'd like them. She, Ben, and his family had filled a void in Gabe's life, and he wanted them to have a home they would love. He wanted to build one where Faith would be able to have her own space even though she'd have boarders. He was anxious to show them to her, but for the last few days, the only neighbors he'd seen had been Ben or Matt as they ran over something to eat or just to check on him and talk for a while.

They were probably as restless as he was.

He grinned as Ben poked his head inside. "Want some company?"

"You know I do. I'm getting a little tired of talking to myself. I've even started to answer."

Ben laughed as he entered the tent and closed the flap. "Sometimes I wish Matt would stop talking, but I guess having no conversation would be worse."

"Believe me, it is."

"I think the rain has let up for a bit. I hope it's for good. Faith and Hope are handling this crazy weather much better that Matt and I are. Faith says it's because they are catching up on mending and knitting and that working with their hands helps, but I think even they are at their wits' end."

Gabe could believe it. He was there himself. "I've been mucking out this tent best I can. Guess you and Matt have been doing the same."

"Oh yeah. An impossible task. At least Faith and Hope are up out of it. She tried to get us to move to the wagon, but for the most part we've been okay. I didn't want to keep bringing more mud into the wagon."

The sudden quiet caught their attention, and Gabe opened up the tent flap. "I do believe we're going to get a break in the weather."

Ben followed him out of the tent to see the clouds breaking up and the sun peeking through. Mud holes were everywhere, but a huge rainbow gave them hope that the rain was over and a better tomorrow was on its way.

"Papa, it's over, isn't it?" Hope said from the wagon.

"I believe it is, Hope."

"Oh, thank You, Lord," Faith said from behind her.

Gabe couldn't see her, but the sound of her voice went straight to his heart and told him that was what he'd been missing most of all.

# eight

Faith was so thankful that the rain had stopped and maybe life could move forward. The wind and dust and then rain of the past week would have been unbearable had it not been for the dream of having her boardinghouse and wondering what kind of plans Gabe had drawn up.

She and Hope got busy cleaning as much as they could around the camp while Ben, Matt, and Gabe mucked out their tents. Later that morning, Ben and Gabe went to see how others had faired and to see if they could be of help. When they returned, Faith was busy preparing a hot meal of buttered potatoes and the fried rabbit Matt had trapped. She had plenty of fresh rainwater in the barrels Ben and Matt had put out to catch the rain.

"It's about ready," Faith said as they walked up.

"Mmm, we could smell that fried rabbit over a block away." Gabe sniffed appreciatively.

"I'm starving," Matt said. "I thought you two would never get back."

"With all the mud in the streets, it was slow going. Didn't see that Frank Jarvis, did you?"

"Nope. Nowhere around here. Maybe the bad weather sent him back to wherever it was he came from," Matt said.

"We can hope so."

"Could well be," Gabe said. "I heard a lot of people high-tailed it out of here once the rain came. One man said the train was as full leaving as it was when it got here."

Ben offered the blessing after Faith had fixed everyone's plate, and she was glad that at least they had stools to sit on that didn't sink too far into the mud. There was silence for a while as each of them took care of their hunger for a hot meal.

"This is so good, Aunt Faith," Matt said. "I was beginnin' to think we'd never have anything but cold biscuits, jerky, and crackers again."

"Glad I made up an extra batch of biscuits the other day, or we wouldn't have had them. Should have fried more bacon, too. But this does taste kind of good, if I do say so myself."

"And you're right to say so." Gabe grinned at her. "I don't know what I'd have done without those biscuits and bacon you gave me. And I thank you for the extra you sent over with Ben and Matt from time to time."

"No thanks needed, Gabe, but you are welcome," Faith said. "You'd have done it for us."

"I heard several families crammed into one lean-to on down close to the center of town and pooled all their food," Ben said.

"Did you check on the Littletons down the way?" Faith had been worrying about Amy ever since the weather turned bad and felt awful that she hadn't checked on her.

"We did. Thankfully, she'd made up extra food like you did, and they did pretty well. Looks like that baby could come any day now, but they sure were glad it didn't come during that wind and rain," Ben said.

"Oh, so am I. I'll go over and check on her tomorrow."

"I'm sure she'd love that. She did ask about everyone."

Faith felt even worse that she hadn't been over to check on Amy. She told herself that she would make a pie to take over to them, soon as she could.

"Have you heard how many people came in with us?" Hope asked.

"Yep. Saw a paper today. They say no less than fifteen thousand people were surrounding the land office that first day, and that was mostly men. There's been all kinds of disputes over lot lines, too," Ben said.

Gabe nodded. "We're hoping one of the government surveyors will get here in the next few days so we can figure out the best location for your house, Faith. I'm about through with the plans I've drawn up. If you'd like to look them over, I can go get them."

"Oh, I'd love to see them."

Gabe put his plate down and stood.

"You don't have to get them right now, Gabe. There's no hurry. You can get them after supper or even tomorrow will be fine. You finish your supper while it's hot."

He sat back down. "Guess I'll do that. Ben's told me that you've been waiting to see what I've come up with, and I wanted to get your opinion on some things before I finish them up."

"You can get them while Hope and I clean up and before we have our pie and coffee. How's that?"

"That's just fine by me. I guess I'm anxious to know what you think of them."

He really sounded a little uncertain as to what she would think, but Faith had no doubt at all that she was going to love the plans he'd drawn up. Excitement bubbled up inside when the last of the rabbit was finally eaten and Gabe headed to his tent to get the plans.

She put a fresh pot of coffee over the fire before she and Hope began to clean up. The moon was up and the stars out when Gabe came back over. Ben lit several lanterns so they could see, and Faith held her breath, waiting to get her first look at what could be their new home.

❧

Gabe waited as Faith looked over his plans. Would she hate them? Like them?

"Oh, Gabe!"

The smile Faith gave him told him all he needed to know, and he let his breath out with a *whoosh*. She liked them.

"These are wonderful. It's as if you read my mind in all I was hoping you would do."

"I can't tell you how happy I am to hear that. Do they need any explaining, or are they clear to you?" He leaned over her and pointed to the first plan, which had one story. "This house has a total of six bedrooms, and it's a nice size, but it won't give you quite as much room for boarders."

"It is very nice though." Her gaze slid to the next paper. "And this one, too. But this one—oh, it's lovely."

Gabe was glad he'd drawn up the elevations along with the plans so that she could see what they might look like from the street. He'd actually drawn up three. The first was a huge sprawling one story that was nice but wouldn't leave much room for a garden. The three story was probably more than she wanted or needed. The two story, the one she said was lovely, was his favorite, and he hoped she'd choose it. It had eight bedrooms, plenty for her family and the boarders she wanted. Once he moved into his own place and Ben found the land he wanted, she'd even have room for their visits and her boarders.

"But. . .well, I'd need to know the cost of each one."

"It's not going to be as much as you think. With free labor, we should be able to build the one story for around $1,250, the two story for around $2,500, and the three story for about $4,000. I know that sounds like a lot but—"

Faith shook her head. "No. Not after what I've seen back East. And with what my husband left me, I believe I can afford it and the furnishings. But if not, surely with it being a place of business, I can get a loan for what I might need."

"Good then," Gabe said. "All you need to do is make up your mind which one is right for you and that you like the best."

Faith looked up at him, and he was rewarded with a huge smile. "You'll not be lacking for business once news of your talent gets out. I know which one I'm leaning toward, but may I keep these overnight to make sure?"

"Thank you, Faith. And of course you may keep them overnight. Those are your copies. I drew several of each so that you'd have your own."

"Thank you, Gabe. I'll try not to take too long with my decision."

"You have time. We've got to make sure where our lot lines are, and we can't do anything until it dries up around here, anyway."

"And now I have my dream to look forward to while we wait. Thank you."

The appreciation in her eyes warmed Gabe's heart. "You're welcome. Just think about how many boarders you might want, what kind of space you'd like for yourself, and what you might want your home to be in the years to come. That will help with your decision making."

She nodded. "That makes sense. I'll do that."

Gabe couldn't help but notice how her gaze kept going from one plan to the other. He was glad he was going to be able to help her dream come true. He'd do the best he could to make her home all she wanted it to be, and he couldn't wait to get started.

But wait they must, he realized as he said his goodnights and dodged mud holes on the way back to his tent. Hopefully, it would stay clear long enough to dry out the ground, and by then they'd know where their lots began and ended.

※

Faith watched Gabe head back to his claim. Her pulse hadn't slowed down since she'd first seen him that day. She'd been surprised to realize how much she'd missed him, how happy she was to see him, and more than a little disturbed by it all. She was going to have to be careful, or she might lose her heart to the man, and she couldn't let that happen. But she could be appreciative of the plans he'd drawn up.

These were every bit as good as the ones drawn up by architects for a summer home for her in-laws. Faith couldn't get enough of looking at them, but she'd known from the first that she would choose the two-story plan. It was all she'd ever dreamed of in a home. The kitchen would be a delight to cook in, and the dining room plenty big enough for boarders and family. The bedrooms were large and airy, and there was even one downstairs, with a sitting room. She'd be able to have some privacy and quiet after a long day of taking care of others.

It was a dream, but one she felt was close to coming true thanks to a husband who cared enough to see that she'd be taken care of if anything happened to him, a brother who knew she needed a new start, and a stranger who'd turned into a friend. She thanked the Lord above for each one and for the blessings He'd given her through them.

When her husband had died in a riding accident over a year ago, Faith had been devastated. She'd missed Noah with every fiber of her being. Then his parents had become unbearable, making it obvious that they hated that she was still with them when their son wasn't, yet unwilling to let her move out on her own because of what their friends would think. All she'd wanted was to get away from them—and all the memories of what could have been had her husband lived.

Now his sweet face was beginning to fade in her memory, and if not for the small photograph of him on their wedding day, she'd soon forget what he looked like. Yet those last few months their relationship had suffered from living in a house on his parents' property, wanting a home of their own, and not being able to have a child of their own.

Her heart ached that she'd never been able to give him a child. What comfort it would be to have their child with her now. But it wasn't to be, and she could do nothing about the fact that she'd been unable to conceive. She was just so thankful that Ben had come up with the answer for her to be able to get away. And she was sure her in-laws were thrilled that her brother had asked for help with his children, giving them an excuse to let her leave.

Now she was on the verge of a new life, and as exciting as it was, she longed to have someone to share it with. But that was a dream that couldn't come true. She had to be on guard never to fall in love again. She couldn't bear disappointing another man because of her inability to have children.

Suddenly, Gabe Logan came to mind, and she shook her head, trying to dismiss his handsome face. It helped only until she looked again at the plans he'd drawn up. They didn't know a lot about him, but he'd been there to help from the moment they met him, first at the river, then when Frank Jarvis accused Ben of stealing his claim. And now this. He was giving her something new to dream about. Gabe Logan was a good man. One a woman could love. And she had to be very careful to make sure that dream of hers didn't include him.

# nine

Gabe went back to his site, pleased that Faith liked his plans so much. The fact that she could see herself in each home meant more to him than he'd let on, because he'd seen her in each and every room as he'd drawn up the plans.

In the kitchens, he'd imagined her humming one of the many hymns she seemed to love, or pulling a roasted chicken out of the oven, or looking out the window he'd placed above the sink.

In the dining rooms, he'd seen her presiding over her table of boarders. In the—he shook his head and sighed. Faith Anderson had become part of each plan, and it didn't matter which one she chose. He'd do his best to make the house he built be something she loved.

He sat up late, his lantern burning low, as he tweaked and added to the designs he'd already given Faith. He worked on each one as if it was the one she wanted, making sure the kitchens were sunny and bright and easy to work in. The parlors and dining rooms in all the plans were roomy, with lots of windows and a fireplace in each.

Gabe laid down the plans, stood up, and stretched. He'd have one last cup of coffee before going to bed. His coffee didn't hold a candle to Faith's, and he was tempted to go over and ask for a cup, but when he looked over, it was to see her and Ben, their heads bent over his plans.

Much as he wished he could be part of their decision-making process, he wasn't. And he wouldn't intrude. He heated up the pot of coffee he'd made earlier in the day and looked at the night sky. There seemed to be a million stars up there, shining down. The moon was large and full, and he hoped they were in for a dry spell—at least long enough to get Faith's boardinghouse built.

He sat down on the barrel of nails he'd had delivered that day and took a sip of the more-than-a-little-strong coffee—hoping it wouldn't keep him awake.

After all that had gone on in his life the last year, it would be good to get back to work. To be part of making someone's dream come true. To build a comfortable home for a family he'd come to care about.

Ben and his wife had done a wonderful job of raising Matt and Hope—they were good kids. He knew Ben would continue on as best he could without his Molly. Faith would help all she could. Her nurturing nature had been apparent from the first time he met her. At least he could still trust his instincts.

Something about that woman made him wish for things he'd given up on. After Laura had died, he'd made up his mind never to fall in love again. But he couldn't stop the longing for a wife and a family to love and care for, even knowing that wasn't something he'd likely ever have.

He knew from the way his chest tightened each time he saw Faith that he was beginning to care about her. But he couldn't let himself fall in love with her. Her kind of woman didn't marry a man who'd spent time in jail—even if he wasn't guilty of the crime. He could well have been.

Faith Anderson wasn't the kind of woman who'd be looking to him as a husband or future father for her children. She was a good Christian woman, and she'd never consider him husband material—not once she found out about his past. He'd best remember that.

Gabe poured out the rest of his coffee and put out his fire before heading to bed. But his heart warmed when he looked over to see Faith's head still bent over his plans, the light from her lamp burning low.

He went back to her house plans feeling lonelier than ever but determined to build the best boardinghouse in the area. At least he could do that for the woman he'd begun to care way too much about, in spite of all his resolves not to.

❧

The next morning, Gabe brought over modified plans. Faith had thought they couldn't get any better than what he'd given her the night before, but they were. Little touches—a pantry right off the kitchen in one, a door down to the cellar from the pantry in another, and a cozy area upstairs where boarders could sit and chat in another. Differences that made each plan even more special. And while each change gave her something to think about, Faith kept leaning toward the two-story concept she'd loved from the first.

"Faith may not know which plan she wants yet, but she's determined to be ready to build as soon as possible," Ben said. "I'm going over to the bank with her after breakfast so she can get money transferred. Will you keep an eye on things?"

"I'd be glad to. Maybe the surveyors will show up today," Gabe said.

"Oh, I hope they do," Faith handed him a plate of bacon and eggs, but she wasn't prepared for the little shock that shot up her arm when her fingers touched his. Her hand began shaking, and if Gabe hadn't grabbed the plate tight, she'd have dropped it.

"I'm sorry. I'm a little shaky today—I could barely sleep last night for thinking about the plans." She hoped he'd think that was the reason she was so clumsy and wouldn't connect it with his nearness. The way her heart flip-flopped each time he smiled at her had to stop. She must get a grip on how she reacted to this man.

"I understand," Gabe said. "I had trouble sleeping, too. It's always that way when I'm drawing up plans. I'm glad you liked them all."

Faith chuckled. "Might have been easier if you'd only given me one choice."

The day seemed to fly by. The people at McNeal and Little Banking Company were very helpful, and it took no time at all to arrange to have the money she'd placed in an Arkansas City bank transferred to Guthrie. She was pleased to see that the bank was now in a frame building instead of a tent.

Faith hadn't been out and about much since the rain had stopped, and she was quite surprised to see the hustle and bustle of a town being born. While most businesses were still working out of tents, more frame buildings were going up than she'd expected.

"Ben, you didn't tell me that several grocers were setting up business already. And look!" She pointed across the street. "There's already a drugstore and"—Faith peered farther down the street—"is that a tiny seamstress shop there beside that dry goods store?"

"That's what the sign says. Looks like two people tried to claim the same lot, and they divided it up. Or maybe the wife is the seamstress and the husband runs the store. Things have been changing around here by the hour, and it's hard to keep up."

It was difficult for Faith to take it all in. Several hotels were going up, and eateries were doing business out of tents—all with long lines of people waiting to get in. The streets were full of all kinds of buggies and wagons, and people were crossing the road willy-nilly to get from one store to another.

Finally, she had a feel for the layout of Guthrie and was kind of glad that her lot wasn't right in the middle of it—more at the edge, but close to everything. She hoped that her boarders would be able to relax at the end of a day and feel at home in her house.

When they reached the Littleton lot, Faith told Ben to go on without her so that she could visit with Amy for a bit. The Littletons were just a block down from Faith's lot, and she'd make her way home fine.

Amy looked ready to have had the baby several days ago, and she seemed more than a little glad to see Faith.

"I'm beginning to think this baby is never going to get here, Faith. I've wanted to come see you, but John has been afraid for me to get more than a few feet away from our wagon. It's so good to see you."

"I'm glad to see you, too. I'll be praying the baby comes soon."

"Did you think the rain would never end? What a mess it's been. But it was such a blessing to see the sun again. What have you all been doing?"

"Well, our neighbor Gabe Logan drew up some plans for the boardinghouse I'm going to start."

"A boardinghouse? What a wonderful idea. I'm sure you'll be full up in no time at all."

"I hope so. If I can decide which plan to choose. I have them with me, if you'd like to look at them."

"Oh, I'd love to."

Faith pulled the plans out of the pocket of her skirt and laid them out so Amy could look at them. She oohed and ahhed for half an hour before she turned to Faith.

"How many boarders are you wanting? Do you really want to

keep up a house this big?" Amy pointed to the three-story plan.

"Not really," Faith admitted. Keeping that large a home clean had been a concern of hers. "If I did well enough, I suppose I could hire extra help, but still, that'd be a lot of people if I was full up."

"And the one-story plan doesn't seem quite large enough for a boardinghouse."

"Exactly."

"Well then, I'd pick the two-story house. It seems to be the one you like the most, and I really think it will fill your needs the best. I especially like that it has a small sitting room just for you. After taking care of so many people all the time, you are going to need some time to yourself."

"I love that, too. But I like everything about the house. The rooms are spacious, there are enough of them, and I love the kitchen. . .and the porches. I can't wait to watch the sun rise and set from them."

"Sounds like you've made your decision."

"It does. But I'll think on it another day or so."

"You know, I really like the one-story house. Do you think John and I could call on Mr. Logan to draw us up some plans?"

"I'm sure he'd be glad to. He's a builder by trade, and the earlier you get on his list, the better. Especially once he starts building on my lot."

"We'll do it." Amy rubbed her growing middle, and her smile was one of anticipation mixed with impatience. "Once this baby gets here, maybe we can get started on our own place."

Faith tried not to show her envy and to count her own blessings. Building her home was first on Gabe's list. That was a big one. "It surely won't be long now before the baby comes."

"I certainly hope not. At least there are a few doctors who've hung out their shingles in the last few days, so I have them to call on if there are any problems."

"I'll be praying all goes well and that you have an easy time, Amy."

"Thank you, Faith. That means a lot. I'm hoping I'm like my mother. She said she never had a hard time. Just a couple of pains and that was it."

But Faith could see the anxiety in Amy's eyes and tried to reassure her. "I hope you are like her, too. Surely you are. You made the trip out here in your condition. That says a lot."

The furrows in Amy's brow faded, and she nodded. "That's true. My mama said she wouldn't have the courage to leave behind all she knew when she was in my condition."

"Well, see then? You'll do fine. But if you should need me, have John come and get me or send for me."

"Thank you, Faith. I do have a neighbor just down the street who's had six children. She said she'd help, too."

"Well, I'm sure you'll be more comfortable with someone who's had experience. I'll help by bringing in some food."

"Oh Faith, I am so glad I met you! Thank you for checking on me and for your friendship. I can't tell you how much it's meant to me to have someone around my age nearby."

"It means a lot to me, too. And thank you for helping me with the house plans." Faith realized that it gave her as much comfort to feel she had a woman friend here as it did Amy.

She headed back to her lot, praying that all went well for her new friend, that the baby would come soon, and that Amy would have an easy time of it. She might never be able to have a child of her own, but she was determined to be happy for anyone who could.

&

By the end of the week, Faith knew she wasn't going to change her mind on which plan she liked the best and decided to tell Gabe which one she'd chosen. At supper, she pulled it out and handed it to him. "This is the one I want you to build. I like them all so much, but this one, I love. I can see me living there a very long time."

She was rewarded with a huge grin and a nod as Gabe looked at the plan she'd chosen. "I like that one the most, too. I pictured you best in that one."

The fact that he'd thought about her living in a house he'd be building pleased her immensely. Faith could feel her face flush with pleasure, and she was alarmed at the way her heart did a funny little twist in her chest, signaling to her that she cared about this man whether she wanted to or not. As she'd looked over the plans, she'd somehow pictured him in the rooms he'd drawn, too, and that wasn't something she could let herself do. Not now. Not ever.

"We all agreed that it was the one," Faith said, trying to ignore the way her pulse raced as Gabe continued to smile at her. "When do you think you can get started?"

"Soon as we have our claims okayed by the surveyors. They should be here any day now."

"Then let me know how much money you need to start ordering supplies, and I'll go to the bank and withdraw that amount or have it transferred to yours, if that would be easier."

Gabe nodded. "I'll start making a list. I know about how much lumber to order. I'll have a list ready for you to take to the bank by tomorrow or the next day."

"Good." Faith fixed their plates, and they settled down to eat the supper of fried chicken, gravy, and biscuits that she'd made. She'd been glad to be able to replenish her staples from one of the new mercantiles a street over. Increasingly, Guthrie felt like a town, even if many of the businesses were set up in large tents.

Faith poured Ben and Gabe another cup of coffee. She was thankful that she still had rainwater to use. Water from the river still needed to be boiled before using.

She liked having someone to cook for again. She'd always loved to cook, but her in-laws had frowned upon her doing it. They'd wanted everyone to believe they were wealthy. It'd been easier to hire someone than to hear their harping about it.

Now she'd be able to do all that her mother had taught her. She'd never quite taken to being idle, and she was glad to keep busy now.

"Look," Matt said, pointing across the street. "Isn't that the Jarvis man who claimed Pa stole his claim?"

Faith, along with Ben and Gabe, turned to look, but by then, the man had turned and was walking in the other direction.

"He'd better not come around here again," Ben said. "Not unless he's looking for trouble."

"I am surprised that he didn't cause more trouble that first day," Faith said.

"He couldn't prove Ben had taken his claim. Plenty of people saw us come in and knew he didn't get here before us. Not unless he got here before they did." Gabe took a swallow of coffee before continuing. "Could be one of those Sooners that came in early."

"More'n likely he did," Ben said. "Maybe the law will catch up to him one of these days."

The very thought of the man sent a familiar shiver down Faith's spine. He might not be causing trouble now, but she had a feeling they hadn't seen the last of him.

# ten

Guthrie seemed to change by the hour, with tents giving way to frame buildings, and some of those beginning to give way to brick ones now that the brickyard had opened up. Supplies streamed in on trains and by freight wagons, and there was beginning to be some semblance of order.

Daily fights still erupted over claims, and Faith was surprised that Jarvis hadn't shown back up with the law, but she thanked the Lord daily and prayed that he never would.

It did her heart good to see grocery stores, drug stores, shoe stores, and even furniture stores popping up all over. Most still in tents, but others already in frame buildings. Faith felt part of something new and wonderful, and she was glad to call Guthrie home. She couldn't wait to open up her boardinghouse.

The surveyors had come and gone, deciding that Faith's and Gabe's lots were both fine, but the lot next to Faith's was now part of a street. The settler was none too happy to be told he had to relocate.

"Why is it me whose got to move? Why not her?" The settler pointed at Faith.

"Sorry, mister," the deputy said. "But the town was laid out in advance of the run, and you're in the middle of the street. There's nothin' we can do about it."

The settler spit onto the street and muttered a string of expletives but finally began to gather up his things, shooting dark looks at Faith all the while.

Faith thanked the Lord daily that Ben had put claim to the lot they were on.

With her lot now on a corner, it would be an even better location for a boardinghouse. And finally, Faith knew she lived on the edge of the city proper of Guthrie, on the corner of Noble and Second streets.

Her lot wasn't far from Cottonwood Creek, which would make it easy to water a garden until a well could be dug to bring water to the house. They'd moved the wagon to the front of the lot—farthest from the corner—to allow easy access for the wagons bringing in supplies, and Gabe and Ben had leveled the land and were close to beginning to frame the house. They'd built an outhouse out back, but once the house was done, there'd be a real bathroom. Actually there'd be two—one upstairs and one downstairs, just for her. Faith still found that hard to believe.

She was so excited she could barely get her work done for either watching everything the men were doing or poring over the Montgomery Ward catalog she'd unearthed from her trunk. Her days were filled with decisions—those Gabe required of her in the building of the boardinghouse and the ones she must make about the furnishings. She hadn't had a chance to look at any of the furniture stores, but hopefully there would be an even better selection by the time she was ready to make her purchases.

She'd been debating whether to put an advertisement in the *Oklahoma State Capital*, the first newspaper in the newly claimed land, and she brought the subject up as they sat down to supper.

"You could probably just put out a sign on the street and have plenty of people ask to be placed on your waiting list," Ben said.

Gabe agreed. "I'm surprised no one has approached you about it yet. We've had a lot of people watching us the last few days."

"Well, more'n likely they just think we're building a home," Ben said.

"Ben's right," Faith said. "The only person I've told about the boardinghouse is Amy Littleton, and she's so busy with the new baby that she probably hasn't told anyone but John."

Gabe took a swig of coffee and nodded. "He came to see me the other day and asked if I'd draw up plans similar to the one-story project you showed his wife. I've been working on them and planned to take them over after supper. Thank you for the good recommendation."

"I didn't have to do anything but show Amy your plans. She liked them all as much as I did and asked if I thought they could approach you to draw up some for them. I told her she should get on your list fast."

"Well so far, they are the only ones on the list."

"Maybe you should put out a sign, too," Faith suggested.

"Maybe so."

"You know, I think I heard that the *Oklahoma State Capital* does all kinds of printing besides the newspaper. Might want to see if they can get those signs made up," Ben suggested.

"I think we should!" Faith clapped her hands together.

"You could have a contest to see who gets the most names on their waiting list," Matt suggested.

"Sounds like fun," Gabe said.

"It does. Let's do it," Faith said.

❧

Their signs went up the next afternoon, and by suppertime Faith had ten names on her list. Gabe had eight, and he didn't care if he ever caught up to her. She was getting more excited by the day.

Gabe had brought over the supplies list, and she'd gone to the bank that day to have the first of the money transferred into his account. He and Ben would be starting the framing soon. It was hard to believe they'd been here nearly a month already.

Faith had invited the Littletons to join them for supper, and Gabe looked forward to talking to them about their plans.

He and Ben had made a table and bought a few chairs, so when the Littletons joined them, everyone could gather around for the meal Faith was preparing for them.

Gabe couldn't help but notice that Faith had a hard time taking her eyes off the couple's newborn as Mrs. Littleton placed her in Faith's arms. He had to admit Lily was a pretty baby. But it was the longing in Faith's eyes as she cuddled the child that caught Gabe's attention.

She wanted a child of her own, and that realization had his heart tightening in his chest and reminded him that his past wasn't the kind a woman wanted in the man she married. But suddenly Faith thrust the baby back into Mrs. Littleton's arms, saying she thought something was burning. It was as if she suddenly couldn't bear to hold the baby, and Gabe wondered why. . . .

"We've made a decision about the plans you drew up for us, Mr. Logan," John Littleton said.

Gabe pulled his gaze from Faith and turned to the man. "Please, just call me Gabe. We're going to be seeing a lot of each other if I'm going to build your home."

"Gabe, then. And I'm John."

"All right, John. Which plan have you chosen?" Gabe

wasn't surprised when the man pulled out the same one-story drawing that he'd drawn up for Faith. It was a good plan and would work for this young couple. "Are there any changes you want?"

"Only a few." The man looked over at his wife and child. "Amy liked the sitting room you gave Faith and thought she'd like one, too. First as a nursery and then, as our children grow, as a sitting room for us."

The love the man had for his wife shone from his eyes, and Gabe's gaze strayed to Faith. How wonderful it would be to—

"Will that be a problem, Gabe?" John drew his attention back to where it belonged.

"No problem at all. In fact that's a very good idea. All it will really take is for me to put a pocket door between your room and the one next to it."

"That's what we thought. Amy will be thrilled when I tell her."

"Please call her over, and we'll see what else she might want that she hasn't told you."

As Faith finished preparing supper with Hope's help, Gabe and the Littletons put the final touches on their house plan, with several suggestions from Ben and Matt.

Gabe felt a certain amount of security knowing that he'd have a paying job coming in soon. He had no intention of charging Faith for his labor. Wouldn't have even if he weren't going to have a place to stay while he worked on his own place. But it was good to feel that he'd be able to begin making a living in this new place he called home.

As they all sat down to eat, Ben said grace. "Father, we thank You for this new life You've given us, for the friends You've brought into our lives, and for all the possibilities

You've put before us. Please watch over us, and guide us each day to do Your will. In Jesus' name. Amen."

As Gabe listened to Ben's prayer, he felt as if the Lord had given him a new beginning here in Guthrie, with people he felt would be lifelong friends and an opportunity to heal from the pain of the past. He felt blessed.

Suddenly, he realized it'd been a long time since he'd talked to the Lord. Really talked to Him. Oh he'd sent up an occasional thank you here and there, but he'd spent more than a little time angry because of Laura's death and all that happened after it, and he'd felt that the Lord had turned His back on him.

But Gabe knew He hadn't. He'd been there all the time— getting him through it all, staying with him when Gabe didn't know if he could or even wanted to go on. Gabe only now realized just how much he'd missed his daily talks with the Lord, and he resolved right then and there never to miss a day again.

Faith, Ben, and the children had been going to church since the first one opened its doors. Maybe he'd join them on Sunday.

As they enjoyed the meal, they talked about Guthrie and how the town government was coming together, how Oklahoma Territory would surely become the next state in the Union.

"This town of ours will most likely become the capitol, don't you think?" John asked.

"I'd say it's a good possibility, from what the papers are saying. Of course Oklahoma City is wanting it bad, too," Ben said.

"That's true. But I think Guthrie has the best chance between the two," Gabe said. He'd been trying to keep up with the news at night. Once he went back to his tent, he didn't have much else to do but read the papers or draw up house or building plans—and try to quit thinking about Faith. He wasn't sure how he was going to handle that once they were under the same roof. He looked over to find her eyes on the Littletons' baby once more, and the look in her eyes had his heart hurting for her.

She'd make a wonderful mother, and Gabe couldn't help but wonder why she'd never had children. Had she lost a child? There'd never been any mention of it, but the look in her eyes. . . It made Gabe want to hold her in his arms until the hurt in them went away.

Once the Littletons took their leave, Faith seemed to relax, convincing Gabe that it was a baby she longed for.

"They are going to try to join us for church in the morning," Faith said. She caught Gabe looking at her and said, "We'd love to have you join us, too. We leave here soon after breakfast."

Was he ready to return to church? He wasn't sure. "I'll sleep on it."

Faith's eyes lit up, and she smiled. "You do that."

He smiled back. If going to church with her would dispel the sadness in her eyes, he'd go for her. . .and for himself.

❧

Faith got ready for church the next morning, trying to put her dreams out of her head. She'd tossed and turned most of the night. In one dream, she was holding a baby, and a feeling of completeness had washed over her. In the next dream, the baby was being taken away from her, and the emptiness of her arms had her waking in tears.

She knew the dreams had been brought on by holding Amy's little one in her arms and by the longing it stirred up in her. But somehow, some way, she had to accept that she would never have a child of her own. For whatever reason, the Lord had decided that she wasn't to have children, and she had to accept His will.

Instead of feeling sorry for herself, Faith needed to thank the Lord for the blessings she did have. She had family that loved her, and she had new friends in her life. She'd be able to see Amy and John's daughter grow up, even if she couldn't have a child of her own. She was going to open a boardinghouse. She was—

"Ready, Faith?" Ben called from outside the wagon.

"I'm ready." Hope had cleaned up after breakfast but still was finished dressing long before Faith, and now everyone waited for her. Faith hurried out and took Ben's helping hand to climb down.

"Are you alright, sis? You were awful quiet at breakfast."

"I'm fine." And she would be. It was a beautiful Sunday, and she would think on all the good things in her life and rejoice in them.

When she saw Gabe striding over in their direction, her heart warmed because he was taking her up on the invitation to join them.

"Thought I'd join you in church this morning," he said.

Her heart did a triple flip as he smiled at her, and Faith was glad when Ben answered for her.

"We'd be glad for you to join us. It's the best way to start a week that I know of."

Gabe only nodded as he fell into step beside them. Faith had wondered if he would ever go to church with them, and now that he was, her heart felt about ready to burst with joy.

Faith never thought any other man would be able to claim her heart after her Noah, but Gabe Logan seemed to be making his own place. And she couldn't let that happen. It would only serve to bring heartache—for she would never marry again.

It wasn't as if she were a normal widow who could give a man a child. In the two years she and Noah had been married, she'd never conceived. It had caused so much strain between them that their marriage hadn't been what it had started out to be. Noah had said it didn't matter, but she knew that it did. Even if he did love her, he was disappointed that she couldn't conceive. His parents had made that very clear after his death. She'd never forget his mother saying, "Noah always wanted a houseful of children, and you couldn't even give him one!"

Faith couldn't go through that pain again. She must learn to be content with what she had and not let herself start yearning for something that could never be.

❧

Gabe knew he'd pleased Faith by going to church with them. He'd seen it in her eyes and the welcoming smile she'd given him. But a hint of sadness shadowed her eyes this morning, and she'd been quiet ever since breakfast. He couldn't help but wonder what was bothering her.

The church was still meeting in a tent, but the members had made or brought in benches, and Gabe didn't have a chance to feel awkward as the singing began before they could take a seat. It wasn't until he sat down that he realized Ben had gone in first, then his children and Faith. Gabe sat down beside her and tried to keep up with the singing. But it'd been awhile since he'd gone to church, and he couldn't quite remember all the words.

Faith nudged him and offered to share her hymnal. He smiled down at her and took hold of the left side of the book while she held the right side. The Littletons joined them in their row of benches, and after they'd all moved closer to give them room, he and Faith were standing close as any married couple in the church. Gabe's chest tightened at her nearness.

He had to admonish himself to pay attention when the preacher began his sermon, and after a few minutes, it wasn't hard. The man spoke to Gabe's heart, talking about the new start everyone was making in Guthrie. He reminded them all that it could also be a new beginning with their relationship to the Lord, quoting Paul from Philippians: "Brethren, I count not myself to have apprehended: but this one thing I do, forgetting those things which are behind, and reaching forth unto those things which are before, I press toward the mark for the prize of the high calling of God in Christ Jesus. Let us therefore, as many as be perfect, be thus minded: and if in any thing ye be otherwise minded, God shall reveal even this unto you."

Gabe bowed his head and silently asked the Lord to forgive him for blaming Him for Laura's death, for drawing away from Him. He asked for help to grow closer to Him, and to go on in this new place God had brought him to. It was a new start, and it was time he put the past behind and pressed on.

By the time the preacher ended his sermon, the invitation was issued, and the last song was sung, Gabe was glad they'd come in early. He turned and saw people standing in the aisles all the way around the tent.

As they made their way outside, stopping to talk to a few people they'd met, Gabe had an idea. It was time he paid back Ben and his family for their hospitality. Once they were outside, he turned to Faith and Ben. "Say, I'd like to treat you all for Sunday dinner. There are several restaurants open in town. Don't know how good they are, but I'd sure like to take you all to one."

"Oh please, can we?" Hope asked. "Aunt Faith deserves a break once in a while."

"My thought exactly," Gabe said.

"That okay with you, sis? You haven't started anything yet, have you?"

"Actually, I haven't. And we'd be glad to take you up on your offer, Gabe. I wonder if we can find the Millers' restaurant."

"The Millers? Seems like I've heard of that one or seen a sign," Gabe said. "Are they friends of yours?"

"Well, we don't know them all that well, but we met them the first night we camped. They were very nice and hoped to open a restaurant here."

"Let's see if we can find it, then."

"I think I remember seeing a sign up this way."

Ben took off, walking between his two children, leaving Gabe and Faith no choice but to follow them. Gabe lightly grasped Faith's elbow to help guide her down the uneven street and was pleased when she smiled up at him.

So much for telling himself he wasn't going to let himself care about this woman. He cared. Plain and simple. All the warnings he'd given himself had been for naught. Gabe's feelings for Faith were growing stronger with each passing day. It appeared he had no control of his heart, and there didn't seem to be a thing he could do about it except live with it and accept the fact that he'd never have a future with her because of his past.

## eleven

The Millers had indeed opened a restaurant in a huge tent right on the main street. Mrs. Miller enveloped Faith, Ben, and the children in a hug as soon as she could get to them. "I've been wondering how you all made it. I've asked around, but no one seemed to have heard anything about you."

"We've been staying pretty close to our claim."

"Oh, I understand that," Mr. Miller said, joining his wife and reaching out to shake hands with Ben, Matt, and Gabe. "We've even had fights over claims break out right here in the café."

Ben introduced Gabe, and Mrs. Miller showed them to a table that had just been vacated. "We've roast beef or fried chicken with potatoes and carrots as a special, although we'll cook 'bout anything we have."

Faith ordered the chicken, and so did Gabe, but the rest of her family chose the beef.

"This will be right out. I'm going to have to get back to the kitchen," Mrs. Miller said. "Business has been so good, I had to hire several cooks right off, but they are still kind of in training to the way I like things done."

Faith chuckled. "I understand."

"I'm hoping that they learn quickly. I'd like to get back to church once in a while. There are just so many men without anyone to cook for them, we can't hardly close. But one of these days when they send for their families, I'm going to close long enough to get to church."

91

"Hopefully, that will be soon."

Mrs. Miller hugged her once more. "When things get a little more settled, we'll have to have some tea and a nice long chat."

"I'd like that," Faith said.

A crash sounded from what Faith assumed was the kitchen in another tent in back of the one they were in, and Mrs. Miller was off like a shot.

"My, I think they chose the right business to open," Ben said.

Gabe nodded. "I've seen the lines of people trying to get in here before. Longer than what waits at some of the others in town."

"They'll be rich in no time," Matt said.

"I don't know about that, but at the very least they'll be able to make a good living," Faith said.

"Sure you don't want to open a café, sis?"

Faith shook her head. "I'll be happy cooking for my boarders. And I want to be able to go to church. I think this is too much business for me."

"I'm glad to hear it," Ben said.

"Besides, we're going to put up the frame on that boarding-house tomorrow," Gabe said.

"Really? Tomorrow?"

"First thing in the morning."

"It's really going to happen. Oh my, I'd better get busy looking over that catalog and placing a few orders." She couldn't stop smiling, not even when their meal came.

The food was very good, but Faith was more than a little pleased when Gabe leaned over and whispered, "You are a much better cook than Mrs. Miller—or at least the cooks she's training. You would have a line clear out of town. Sure you don't want me to change those plans?"

She could tell he was teasing and asked, "Then where would you stay until you build your own place?"

He grinned and appeared to be mulling that thought over before saying, "There is that. I believe you've made the right decision."

So did she. And she couldn't wait to see Gabe begin to build her home.

❧

Over the next few weeks, it seemed to take Faith twice as long as ever to get her work done. Even with Hope's help, she struggled to get the wash done, to plan and cook the meals. All she really wanted to do was watch her boardinghouse go up.

She couldn't wait for each morning to begin so that she could see the changes that day would bring. As soon as breakfast was over, she'd pour Gabe another cup of coffee, and he'd walk her through what they were planning on getting done that day.

The outside frame had gone up, and the roof was on, and they'd just finished up the staircases so she could get to the second floor and the attic.

"We're going to start getting the rest of the walls up today," Gabe said as they walked inside.

"Oh, wonderful! I've looked over the plans each night, and I know where each room is supposed to be, but I just haven't been able to get a real feel for the layout yet."

"By tonight you'll have a much better idea. Has the wallpaper you ordered come in yet?"

"No, but I've been told it should be in this week. You aren't ready for it yet, are you?"

Gabe had just taken a sip of coffee, and his chocolate brown eyes looked at her from over the rim of the cup. They reminded Faith of the fudge she loved to make, just before the gloss went off of it.

He was smiling when he lowered the cup. "Not yet. But maybe next week." They walked through what Faith knew was the hall and turned to the left. "You know this is going to be the kitchen, and over there is the dining room, right?"

"Yes, I do know that much, as you well know." He'd pointed those two rooms out to her each time she came over. "One would think those were the most important rooms in the house, Gabe."

Gabe chuckled. "Well, you will be spending a lot of time in both of them. And for a hungry man, they are pretty important."

"True."

"I can't wait to taste what you can create with a range. Have you ordered it yet?"

She shook her head. "Not yet. But I'm going to tomorrow. I want you and Ben to help me decide tonight."

"We can do that."

Footsteps echoed in the hallway, and they turned to see Ben grinning at them. "Are we going to work today, or what?"

"We are. I was just showing your sister what we did yesterday."

"It's looking good, isn't it, sis?"

"She can't quite see the rooms yet. I told her we'd take care of that today."

"We'd better get to work then," Ben said.

"I'll go. I have work to do, too, you know," Faith said. "Besides, the sooner you get to work, the sooner I can feel the flow of the house."

"What's for supper?" Ben asked.

Faith thought for a moment. "If Matt can catch me a few

fish, I'll fry them up and make some cornbread to go with it. If not, it'll be roast chicken and biscuits. How's that?"

"By the end of the day, either one sounds good to me," Ben said.

"Me, too. But that fish would be mighty tasty."

"I'll get Matt on it after the noon meal," Faith said. She was pretty sure he'd be able to catch some. He'd mentioned that the fish were biting the night before. He'd seen several people bringing them in for supper. But he wanted to help Ben and Gabe, too, so they'd decided he could work with them mornings and help Faith of an afternoon.

As she couldn't really see what was going on now that they were inside the house, she was better able to get her work done. After washing up the breakfast dishes, she and Hope went to several mercantiles to look at their selections of ranges. If she could find one in town, she wouldn't have to wait for it to come by rail, and it would be here whenever Gabe had things ready for it.

She was very pleased when she found a selection of Glenwood ranges. The one she liked the best was called the Glenwood Home Grand. It was beautiful and plenty big enough for all the cooking she would be doing in her boardinghouse.

"Oh, Aunt Faith. It's huge. And so new and shiny!" Hope said, opening and closing the oven and looking at the water reservoir.

"It would be perfect for the boardinghouse, wouldn't it?"

Her niece smiled and nodded. "I can almost smell the cakes and pies you could bake in it."

The proprietor had a flyer about it for Faith to take back and show Gabe and Ben. She wasn't sure they knew as much as she did about ranges, but she knew they would love giving their opinions. She ran a hand over it one more time before she and Hope headed back to the claim.

They'd just come out of the store when Hope grabbed her arm. "Aunt Faith, isn't that man that Jarvis person that lied about Papa?" She pointed across the street.

It looked like Frank Jarvis from the side. But when he turned to face them, Faith breathed a sigh of relief. "No, dear. That's not him."

"Oh good. I sure hope he never comes back."

"So do I, Hope."

"I'm glad Papa and Mr. Gabe are working on the boardinghouse, aren't you? I don't worry so much about that Jarvis person when they're nearby."

"Neither do I, Hope. I'm glad they're close at hand." But they wouldn't always be.

"Mr. Gabe sure is a handsome man, Aunt Faith. I catch him looking at you an awful lot."

Faith's pulses quickened. "Do you?"

Hope grinned. "Yes. Even more than I catch *you* looking at him."

Her heart seemed to plummet to her stomach. "Oh Hope! Do you think he notices?"

"I don't know, but would it hurt if he did?"

"Well, I—"

"I don't see how it could. You two sure would make a nice-looking couple."

"Oh Hope, what an imagination you have. Come on now. We need to get lunch ready. They're probably starving by now." Faith hurried her niece along, hoping to put an end to the conversation. But she couldn't get Hope's words out of her mind.

When they got back to the lot, she hurriedly heated up

some of the stew she'd made the night before just in time to serve it when Ben, Gabe, and Matt broke for lunch. They were very appreciative that she was dishing it up for them as soon as they got to the wagon.

"I hope Matt can catch some fish this afternoon."

"Oh, I will. If not, I'll bring in some chicken or quail. I've seen a lot of them lately."

They'd had meat every night for supper since it had stopped raining, and the men said the hunting was the best they'd ever seen. It was a fertile new land they'd come to, and Faith couldn't wait to start her garden, although the end of May might be a little late to begin one. But she'd give it a try. Maybe she could set Matt to work preparing the ground the next day.

The men didn't tarry over their meal. Instead, they hurried back to the house as soon as they were done eating, promising Faith that she would be pleased when she made her next inspection of their work.

She and Hope made quick work of washing dishes. Then they went to visit Amy and the new baby. Faith couldn't wait to tell her how work was going on the boardinghouse, and she couldn't wait to see little Lily. Bittersweet as the experience was, Faith had come to love holding the baby. If she couldn't have her own child, at least she could cuddle Amy's little girl. Lily could grow up to think of Faith as an aunt of sorts, and she'd settle for that.

❧

It was the aroma of fried fish that had Gabe and Ben calling it a day. True to his word, Matt had brought back plenty of fish for supper. Fried golden and crispy, it fairly melted in the mouth. Faith had made cornbread to go with it, and the meal was a real treat after a hard day of work.

Gabe hoped it'd still be light enough for Faith to see what they'd accomplished that day. She'd surely be able to feel the flow of her home after this week.

"I'm surprised you didn't come supervise us today, sis," Ben popped a bite of fish into his mouth.

"I know my limits, Ben. I know nothing about building. . . just what I want in a house. Did you get all the walls up yet?"

"You're kidding, right?" Gabe asked. "We have the walls up in part of the downstairs. Should have them all up by the end of the week. We've hired a couple of helpers to start tomorrow. They came by and asked for work, and well, I'm going to be needing workers to help with the other homes. I figured I might as well hire some good workers before all the ones who know what they are doing are hired out from under me."

"They know what they're doing, that's for sure," Ben said. "By the time we get through, I might know enough to put up my own place."

"We're going to need a brick mason, too," Gabe said. "I'll go to the brickyard and see if they can recommend someone."

"I didn't know we were going to use brick," Faith said.

"Just for trimming out the porch. I want your boarding-house to look as good as some of those rich people's homes going up over on East Noble."

"Thank you, Gabe. I think it's going to be a fine house, with or without brick trim."

"I'll do my best to make it one. If there is enough light after we eat, we can go over so you can see the walls that are up. Maybe you'll begin to see it as home."

"When will you be ready to put in the range? I think I found one here in town." She pulled a flyer out of her apron pocket and handed it to him. "I wanted to see what you and

Ben think about it before I actually buy it."

"You won't have to order it?"

"I don't think so. Not unless someone buys it before I do."

Gabe looked at the range. It should be plenty big enough for the demands of a boardinghouse. Other than that, Faith knew her needs better than he did. "It looks fine to me. We can put it in whenever you want us to."

He handed the flyer to Ben, who promptly handed it back to Faith. "This decision is strictly yours, sis."

"Then I'll buy it tomorrow."

"See if they'll deliver it," Gabe said.

"I'm sure they will. They advertise free delivery." Faith couldn't wait to see it in the kitchen once the walls were up. "Can we go over to the house? The sun isn't all the way down, and I can take a lantern."

"Let's go," Gabe said.

Faith didn't worry about cleaning up first. She jumped up, grabbed a lantern and match, and said, "I'm ready."

"I'll stay here and supervise Hope and Matt while they clean up, sis. Take your time."

Gabe lit the lantern before they entered the house.

"Oh, I can see it now." Faith put a hand to her mouth as she stopped in the hall and looked into the parlor and then turned and walked into the dining room. She turned back to him, and Gabe could see that she was pleased.

Faith noticed the switch on the wall. "What is this?"

Gabe grinned. "Electric lighting will be here before long. The city council is already looking into it. I went ahead and wired the house so that you'll be able to switch it on when it's available."

"That had to make more work for you, Gabe."

"Less work now than later. I learned how to pre-wire back

in Kansas. It will save a lot of time in the long run."

"Electric lights. I thought it would be years before that came to Guthrie."

"People planned for this city long before the land run, Faith. You won't recognize it a year or so from now."

"It's exciting to see a town spring up so quickly, isn't it?"

"It is. So are you beginning to feel the flow of the rooms now?" Gabe asked.

"Oh yes. It feels like a house now." She went through the dining room to the kitchen, where the last of the sunlight shone through the window. "I can't wait to get the range and an icebox in here."

Gabe led her through the kitchen door, back into the hallway, and then down to the second parlor and over into the room that would be hers. It had corner windows so the room would be light and bright all day. "Oh Gabe. I don't know what to say. It's lovely, and it feels like home to me already."

"You couldn't say anything that would mean more to me. I hope you'll like the upstairs as well. We'll get on it tomorrow and be ready to put the pocket doors in as soon as they get here. Pretty soon we'll be hanging that wallpaper for you."

"It won't be long until we'll all have a real roof over our heads once more," Faith said.

"If the good weather holds, you'll be moving in before you know it."

"I'm praying for that good weather and for all to go smoothly for you. And for you to have much success in Guthrie, Gabe."

His chest tightened at the thought that she prayed for him, and his heart seemed to warm at the sincerity in her tone. "Thank you, Faith. I appreciate your prayers. And I'm very glad that you like your new home."

"I don't just like it, Gabe. I love it. I can't think of anywhere I'd rather live. Now I can imagine where to place things, how it will look—I can't wait for it to really become home for others."

The fact that he'd be one of those others for at least awhile made Gabe want to hurry and get finished, too. He couldn't think of anywhere he'd rather live.

❧

Faith and Gabe were just returning to the wagon when Matt came running up. "Papa, Mr. Gabe, it sounds as if someone is at the back of our lot, digging."

"Probably just some animal, but we'd better check it out," Gabe said, hurrying over to his lot to get his shotgun. Ben had his in hand and had turned to Faith before he started to the back of the lot. "You and Hope stay up here, and get that pistol of yours out."

"It's right here." Faith patted her apron pocket. She'd started carrying it once more ever since they thought they'd seen Frank Jarvis again.

"What do you think it is, Aunt Faith?" Hope asked.

"Probably just an animal like Gabe said. Sound carries in the quiet of the evening, so it probably sounded worse that it was."

Hope nodded. "I'll be glad when we get to move into the house. I don't much like sleeping in the wagon."

"I know. It won't be long now. You're going to love it. I can't wait until we can get upstairs and I can show you your room."

Hope grinned. "I can't wait to see it. How long do you think we can keep Papa in town before he starts to look for that land he wants? I really want to stay in town, Aunt Faith."

Faith pulled her close. "Oh sweetie, I know. I'm hoping

we can keep him here for a while. . .hopefully long enough for him to decide he'll stay. But if he decides to move on, maybe I can convince him that you and Matt need to be here for school. Could be we can arrange for you to stay with me during the school year and with him in the summer. What do you think of that?"

"I'd rather just stay here all the time. But I don't want Papa to be by himself either."

Faith sighed. "I know. Neither do I." The thought of Ben being all alone gave her a heavy heart. She wished he'd decide he liked living in town. For his sake, for his children's sake, and for hers.

"It must have been an animal of some sort," Gabe said as he, Ben, and Matt came back from their investigation.

"It might have been on that lot behind us. Just sounded closer, I guess," Matt said.

"Well as long as you didn't run into Jarvis out there, we can rest peacefully tonight," Faith said. She hoped her words were true.

# twelve

The landscape of Guthrie was changing as fast as Faith's house was going up. Buildings replaced more and more tents, and day by day Faith's house turned into a home.

Some claimants, like the one next to Faith, had to be ordered to evacuate their claims because they were in the middle of a city street, and there'd been arguments on the streets themselves.

With all that going on, a huge outcry rose up for the elections of a new city council, and another election was being held the next day, June 3. Voters had many complaints about the new taxes on businesses and even more against the arbitration boards.

While the actions of the boards awarding title certificates to claimants solved many of the disputes, other problems developed between the City of Guthrie and some of the deputy marshals. Both the city and the marshals had been awarding property, and on many occasions they'd given the same parcel of land to two different people, causing major disputes.

Trouble was, too many people were in charge of the same things. With all the planning that went into having the railway in place, mapping out the city, and having federal troops there to keep order, no real planning had gone into governing the city. Federal marshals, the city council, and its city marshal offices were all handling some of the same complaints. It was no wonder problems arose.

Faith hoped the new elections would take care of all the

confusion around them. The complaints had gotten so bad that out of the original seventeen councilmen, only three incumbents—four counting Mayor Dyer—sought to keep their office.

All the talk at supper seemed to center around who to vote for.

"Well, while I'm prepared to vote for Dyer for mayor again, I'm all for getting new people in the city council, and I'm very glad most of the council members decided not to run in this election," Ben said.

"Oh, I agree." Gabe nodded. "But you have to admit that a lot has been accomplished in a short amount of time. We have a bridge across Cottonwood Creek, a water system started, and electricity will be next."

"And yet there's been so much confusion and they've had so many complaints that it's a wonder they haven't already resigned," Faith said.

"I know I certainly wouldn't want the job."

"Really?" Matt said. "I think it would be nice to be elected to an office."

"You'd like to be part of politics, son?"

"Well, not for the sake of politics, Papa, but to help see a town grow and to help the people realize their dreams."

"Hmm," Ben said. "That might take some schooling."

"I suppose," Matt said.

"Now that we have a Citizens School Committee, hopefully they'll be opening up some schools. The newspapers say more than two hundred school-aged children live here."

"Now, Aunt Faith, they don't need to rush," Matt said with a grin. "There's plenty of time for that."

"Besides, its summer," Hope said. "And you are going to need help getting the boardinghouse ready."

"Oh, she'll have that done long before a school session starts, Hope," Ben said.

Both Hope and Matt moaned and shook their heads. But Faith had a feeling they really wouldn't mind getting back to their schooling. In the meantime, there would be plenty to do to keep them busy.

"Yep. By the end of the month, we can start moving those bedsteads and wardrobes upstairs and get them out of the dining room, so Faith can have the furniture for that room delivered."

They'd finally have a real roof over their heads again. She couldn't wait.

੨੶

By the last Saturday of June, everyone was still talking about the election results and how well the new city council seemed to be doing. Mayor Dyer retained his seat, as did Councilmen Howard, Ross, and Sargent. Everyone else was new and had high hopes that the city government would run more smoothly. But many people complained about the arbitration boards and the way they handled claims.

It seemed to be all everyone was talking about, but as interested in the elections as Faith was, nothing was more exciting than seeing her home finally come together and beginning to move in. Hope had been a great help with some of the decorating decisions, and Faith was glad her niece had wanted to give her opinions. Faith wanted this to feel like home for both Hope and Matt.

Wallpaper had been hung in all the rooms; the bedsteads were in the bedrooms, spread with quilts or comforters, each in a different pattern; and crisp curtains were hung in the windows.

With wardrobes, a rocker, and a small writing desk and

chair in each room, Faith felt her family and her boarders would feel they had a place to call home.

The parlors, both the large one and her small sitting room, were furnished with new parlor suites. She'd bought extra chairs to match the five-piece set she'd ordered, to make sure there'd be plenty of room for family and boarders.

Faith had hung more formal draperies in the parlor and dining room, a deep burgundy to match the parlor suite for the parlor, and a gold and burgundy stripe for the dining room. In her small sitting room, she'd ordered a small three-piece set in a deep blue that looked beautiful with the yellow and blue wallpaper she'd chosen for her rooms.

Hope had chosen lavender and pink wallpaper for hers, and she loved it. Matt and Ben had left the décor for their rooms up to Faith, and of course the rest of the rooms would be for boarders, so she tried to choose patterns that would appeal to either men or women.

For the dining room, Faith had found a table large enough to accommodate twelve easily, with a sideboard to match, both at A. J. Spegel's over on Oklahoma and First. The dining room would feel too large without boarders to help fill out the empty spaces, but they'd be moving in soon enough. Before then, her family and Gabe could eat at the smaller round table she'd put in the kitchen.

Moving day had her family and Gabe busy arranging furniture and finally bringing in their belongings. Ben had insisted that he and Matt would share a room, and Faith had given all of them corner rooms. The room she gave Gabe looked out onto his lot so he'd be able to keep an eye on things when he wasn't over there.

Faith was anxious to see what he thought as she opened the door and gave him a key to it. She'd chosen a yellow and burgundy wallpaper and put a striped coverlet of the same colors on the bed.

"My, this feels cozy, Faith. I hope I can make my own place feel this nice."

"Thank you, Gabe. I hope my boarders feel the same way. I wanted to have a little time to get used to where everything is before they settle in, but the first of them will be moving in on Saturday."

"I don't believe you'll ever lack for boarders, Faith. This house is very homey, and I know how well you cook. You'll always have a waiting list."

"Well, this house reflects your craftsmanship, and I love it. It's all I wanted and more, and I really don't know how to thank you."

"You just did. And if that wasn't enough, you are letting me stay here until I get my own place ready."

"There's no hurry for that either, Gabe. Concentrate on getting your office finished and your business up and going. You'll have a place here as long as you need it." Feeling she'd said too much and given her growing feelings for the man away, Faith backed out of the doorway. "I'm going to check on supper. It will be nice to eat at a real table again."

"Yes, ma'am, it will. And whatever you are cooking smells wonderful. The aroma fairly floats up the staircase."

"I hope it tastes as good. But I'm saving it for a surprise. We'll eat at six."

Gabe grinned at her. "I'll be there."

Faith hurried downstairs, hoping she got away before Gabe saw the warm color she could feel creeping up her neck onto her face. She could find no way to express how thankful she was that he'd taken on building her home. Everywhere she looked, she saw special touches that he'd added. She'd paid him for the materials and tried to pay for his labor, but he wouldn't take it. And he wouldn't take any money to pay the extra help he'd hired. He said Ben had paid for that, but she had a feeling about that and determined to ask her brother about it later.

She'd meant it when she'd said he could stay here as long as he needed to. It was the only way she could pay him back for all he'd done. She tried not to think about how good it felt to be able to provide him a home. The only place she had to make sure he didn't make his home in was her heart.

❧

Gabe settled in his room thinking how hard Faith had worked in the last few weeks to make the house he'd built feel like home for anyone who was fortunate enough to live there. He couldn't think of a house he'd built that gave him more satisfaction than this one did. He felt blessed that he would be able to call it home, even if for just a little while. It didn't take long for him to settle into the room. It was the nicest he'd ever had, and Faith had tried to make sure he'd be comfortable in it. And he would be. She'd see to it.

Looking out the window that faced downtown Guthrie, it was exciting to see the growth. Fewer tents now filled the area, and he could see many more frame buildings. By the end of the year, many of those would give way to brick ones.

He'd finished this house, but he had plenty of work waiting for him. He thought he'd take Faith up on her offer to stay here as long as he needed to. Maybe he'd just set up a small office so that he could begin work on other homes. He was hoping to convince Ben to help him, and Matt, too. Both had a natural talent for building, and they were about as hard of workers as he'd come across.

He'd start on his office on Monday, and then he'd be in

business. First up was the Littletons'. John worked for the railroad, so he wouldn't be able to help out, but he'd seen Faith's home and said he trusted Gabe to do the work.

Two other families were waiting, too, and it felt good to be part of this growing town. Good to have a fresh start. It especially felt good to have a room in Faith Anderson's boardinghouse.

Faith had bought a dinner bell so that her boarders would know when to come to the table, and he'd hung it in the hall just outside the kitchen. His stomach was very glad to hear it ring, signaling that supper was ready.

He met Ben and Matt in the upper hallway, and they went down together.

Hope was just putting a bowl of creamed potatoes on the table when they entered the kitchen. The wonderful aroma they'd smelled all day came from a large cut of beef with onions and carrots. Along with peas and hot rolls, it was a meal anyone would be more than glad to sit down to.

Gabe held out a chair for Faith, and Ben said the blessing. Then Faith began handing dishes around the table. He was glad she'd put this table in here. It was just the right size for the five of them, and it would still be a nice place for Faith to have a cup of tea or coffee while she was planning a meal or visiting with Amy Littleton or any other friends she'd be making. Perhaps some of the lady boarders would want to visit with her here as well.

"I love this house, Aunt Faith," Hope said. "It feels so good to get our things out of the wagon and have some privacy."

"I'm not too concerned with the privacy. . . . I don't mind bunking with Papa, but it's nice to have room to stand up and stretch in and to just have a place to sit," Matt added.

Faith had put two chairs in their room, one for each of

them. She seemed to think of what each might need, and Gabe was sure that if she thought a boarder had a special need, she'd find a way to supply it.

He hoped she'd find her rooms as comfortable as she'd made everyone else's. He'd wanted her to have a place for peace and quiet at the end of the day. While they were moving things around, he'd noticed that she'd placed her Bible on the small table beside her bed. It looked worn and loved. He'd placed his less-used one beside his bed, too. One day, maybe it would look as well used as Faith's did.

"What are you going to do next, Gabe?" Ben asked.

"Well, I'd like to get my office up. Then I'll start on the Littletons' place. I was hoping that you would help me with that."

"I suppose I could do that." Ben grinned. "Most people are going to want to wait until harvest to see how they do, now. I figure I can stay until after then."

"I'd sure appreciate it if you would. And I'll pay you, of course. Matt, too, if he wants to help."

"Oh Papa, I'd like to do that."

"Might as well. At least until school starts," Ben said.

"Oh, I'm glad," Faith said. "I've felt bad about taking up all of Gabe's time when I know he's got so many people wanting him to build for them, too."

"No need to feel bad. Your boardinghouse going up is what got me other clients. I wouldn't have been able to make those connections without you."

"Oh, I think you would have. Everyone is looking for a builder."

"I hear a famous one has moved here," Gabe said. "A Mr. Joseph Foucart. I hear tell he trained under the chief architect to the King of Belgium."

"Well, if that's the case, I'm sure he won't be building boardinghouses. . .more like larger buildings, I'd say." Ben chuckled. "Wonder why he came here to Guthrie?"

"I don't know. But I'm sure that nothing he could build would come close to pleasing me as much as this house. And the fact that you and Matt helped Gabe build it means even more."

Faith's smile and sigh, along with her words, warmed Gabe's heart. She was one of the most encouraging women he'd ever met. "I'm glad you are happy with it. I'm sure Mr. Foucart could have designed you something more fancy though."

She laughed. "Gabe, I don't think I could afford this Mr. Foucart from what you say. I imagine the town of Guthrie will have many buildings designed by him, but I like the one a Mr. Gabe Logan designed and built just fine. I don't believe he charged enough."

"Oh yes, he did," Gabe said. "I think I'll take you up on your offer to just build my office and stay here for a little while, if that will make you feel any better. That way I can get started on the Littletons' place a little sooner."

"Oh, that will make me feel better," Faith said. "And I know Amy will be thrilled to get into a house."

Gabe turned to find Ben's gaze going from him to Faith and back again. He had a smile on his face when he nodded and said, "I think that's a good idea, too. No sense in you setting up housekeeping on your own just yet, my friend. You can do that once you catch up with your commitments."

Faith surprised them all with a five-layer cake she'd somehow found time to make that afternoon. "I had to see if I remembered how to bake in a real oven again. My boarders are going to expect desserts."

"Well, I don't know what your last one tasted like"—Gabe forked another piece of cake—"but I'd say you remember quite well. I don't see how it could taste any better than this."

The family added their agreement, and Faith's smile was all the thanks needed.

"It's not bad, if I do say so myself." She took a second bite. "I'm glad you all like it."

Gabe and Ben had a second cup of coffee while Hope helped Faith clean up after supper, and Gabe was reminded of his childhood and how he loved being in his mother's kitchen. He hadn't felt that way in years. This family had taken him in, and he would be forever grateful to them.

He sketched out a plan for his office, making it two stories so that it would be easy to finish out an apartment for himself later, when he had more time. While Faith and Hope worked, he, Ben, and Matt made plans to start work on Monday.

But the next day was the Lord's, and Gabe had come to look forward to going to church with this family. He watched Faith hang up her apron and look around her new kitchen. His heart swelled with a feeling he recognized but couldn't voice. It was enough for now just to know she was happy.

It'd been a long day, and by the time they all decided to retire for the night, Gabe knew he'd sleep well. Not only because he was tired but also because for the first time in a very long time, he felt at home. And by the time he put his head on his pillow, Gabe knew that what made this house a home to him wasn't the furnishings, nice as they were. It wasn't the enticing aromas filling every corner of the house. No, it was plain and simple. All it really took to make this house feel like home was the presence of Faith Anderson.

Building this house for her had been a labor of love, but he didn't think he'd ever feel free to tell her so.

&

Faith was so happy she wondered if she'd be able to sleep. She loved this home more every hour she was in it. She loved the floors, the walls, the staircase, and the kitchen. She loved the pantry and the cellar off the kitchen. She was happy with all of it. But most of all, she loved the rooms she called her own.

Close to the kitchen and downstairs so that she could get up early in the morning or even in the middle of the night and not disturb her boarders or family, she felt as if she had the whole downstairs to herself once everyone went up to bed. She even had her own bathroom.

Gabe had thought of everything. She would make sure everyone she met knew who had built her such a fine boardinghouse. And she had no doubt that it was the nicest in town. She'd made sure to look up her competition, and so far it was mostly hotels. Just a few other boardinghouses had opened up, and they didn't compare to hers. They weren't near as large or as modern as hers. And if she did think so herself, they just weren't as homey.

She'd let her boarders know they could begin moving in the next weekend. She intended to just enjoy her home until then. She wanted Ben and his children to feel like this was their home. Gabe, too, although she tried to dismiss that thought quickly.

It had felt wonderful to gather around the kitchen table with her family after sitting around a campfire for so long. Wonderful to have Gabe right there with them. Whether she wanted to admit how she felt about Gabe or not, she prayed his business would thrive and he'd be able to make a good living for himself.

Faith got ready for bed. Still too excited to sleep, she picked up her Bible and went to her sitting room. Her very own. She still couldn't quite believe it. She sat down on the settee and turned her lamp up so that she could read. It seemed appropriate to be reading about being still and knowing that God is God. This was her quiet place to do that. Faith thanked God for sending Gabe to build it for her, and she especially thanked God for always being with her. She asked Him to bless her family and Gabe all the days of their lives. She couldn't wait to sit in church the next morning and sing praises to His name.

## thirteen

Faith was glad they'd had near a week in the house before her boarders began moving in on Saturday. It truly felt like home. She loved serving her family and Gabe in the kitchen, and the room felt even more special to her because they'd used it.

It was the gathering place. At the end of the day, the men came in through the back door. On the rare occasions she hadn't been in the kitchen or nearby, they seemed to be disappointed and called her name to find out where she was.

She had learned how her range cooked and was very happy with the one she'd chosen. It was easy to operate, and everything she'd cooked had come out wonderful.

It had been so different having everyone come down to the kitchen—sometimes Gabe got there before anyone else and kept her company while she cooked. He seemed to like watching her work in the kitchen, and she liked having him there.

He'd taken to making sure she had plenty of wood each night before bedtime, and he filled the water reservoir in the range so that she didn't have to lift the heavy bucket to do it. Ben had almost stopped checking to see if he needed to replenish the wood box or the water.

She'd only have one room left when her last boarder moved in later that day, and Faith wasn't sure she wanted to fill it yet. With her family and Gabe taking up four rooms and with two couples and one gentleman taking up three more, she'd see how well she could handle taking care of the needs of ten people before adding another.

Mr. and Mrs. Warner had opened a shoe store downtown and were waiting for their home to be built, so they would be leaving after a month or two. But Mr. and Mrs. Fairmont were still trying to decide if they wanted to stay in Guthrie. They'd lost many of their possessions in the run and then seen their claim disappear when told they were in the middle of a street. While they had a half-claim to set up his barber shop, they weren't sure whether to find a lot for a home or build an apartment above their shop if they did stay. For now, Mrs. Fairmont just wanted to be able to think about it without camping in the shop.

Mr. Harrington was a druggist and engaged to a young lady back East. He wanted to be assured he could make a living before going to get her and bring her back. Or rather, as he clarified things, her parents wanted to make sure he could make a living for her before they agreed to let her marry him. He was just glad to have a place to call home and not have to worry about eating out or cooking his own meals.

He was the last to arrive and was quite pleased with the room Faith gave him. "This will work just fine, Miss Anderson. Thank you. I will write home tonight that I'll be well taken care of here until my Mindy can join me and we can get married. Would we be able to stay here once we are married—until we can build a home?"

"Certainly. And just so you know, Mr. Logan, who is staying here also, built my home."

"Really? Well, I must talk to him."

"You'll have plenty of opportunity, I'm sure. Supper is at six thirty."

"Thank you. I'll be on time. Whatever we're having smells wonderful."

"We're having a family favorite of chicken and dumplings, and I'd better get back to the kitchen to make sure it doesn't burn. You saw the dining room and the parlor when you came in. I'll ring the bell when it's time to gather in the dining room."

Faith hurried downstairs and was relieved to find her dumplings were perfect, simmering slowly on a back burner. She was serving green beans with the filling main dish, and Hope had made a berry cobbler for dessert. She certainly hoped her boarders weren't fussy eaters.

When everything was ready, she only had to ring the bell once. She could hear footsteps coming from all directions. She assigned seats to everyone, with her brother at one end and her at the other. Ben had insisted that if he was sitting at the far end from the kitchen, Gabe should take the seat to her right so they could keep heavy dishes moving

She made introductions all around and was happy to find that her boarders weren't picky. Mrs. Fairmont was thin as a rail and just didn't eat much at all. But what she didn't eat, her husband made up for.

"This is mighty good food, Miss Anderson. I do believe we've found the perfect place to stay, dear," he said to his wife.

"I believe you are right, dear." Mrs. Fairmont turned to Faith. "I'm not much of a cook, Miss Anderson. Thank you for providing two chairs in our room. It is such a comfort to be out of the back of that shop and in such a nice big room."

"I'm glad you feel comfortable here. I hope you all will be. As I told you earlier, breakfast will be served from six thirty until eight thirty, the midday meal at twelve noon, and supper will be at six thirty from now on. Sundays, there will be breakfast and Sunday dinner after church. Supper will be light."

All of her boarders seemed agreeable to the schedule, and she breathed a sigh of relief. After all the planning for the boardinghouse, she was a little overwhelmed that she would be responsible for keeping these nice people well fed and comfortable. Thankfully Guthrie had more than one laundry, and she'd told them upfront that they'd have to arrange for their laundry to be done—all except for their linens and bath towels. She'd manage. She hoped.

⋅৯⋅

By the end of the second week of being the proprietor of a boardinghouse, and even with Hope's assistance, Faith knew she needed to hire someone to help them. If she hadn't realized it, her family certainly did.

"Be prepared to have people call on you today, sis," Ben said as he came down to the kitchen on Tuesday morning. "Yesterday, I placed an advertisement in several of the local papers for someone to help you. It should be in today's papers."

"Ben! You shouldn't have done that. And why didn't you tell me last night?"

"You'd just have worried yourself, and me, about it all evening. But you can't keep going at this pace for much longer. You look exhausted all the time, and Hope's not going to be able to help as much once school starts. If you can't enjoy having boarders without it wearing you out, I'm not sure I can leave Matt and Hope with you when I decide to find my own place. I want you to enjoy life a little more, Faith. You deserve it."

"But Ben, I don't know if I can afford—"

"I said the pay would be room and board. You have the one extra room. Might as well use it to your benefit. You don't have to hire anyone you don't think will work, but you really need to interview whoever answers the ad."

"I suppose I could use some more help."

"Sis, you need to do something before your boarders begin to think you don't want them here. Even Gabe has noticed the dark circles under your eyes and the fact that you can barely keep your eyes open to get the kitchen cleaned up and preparations for the next day finished."

"He said something to you?"

"He doesn't like to see you so tired. He's been thinking maybe he ought to move out so you'd have one less room to clean and—"

"No! I can't let that happen. We owe him so much. . . ."

"Well, then just hire someone to help. That should take care of the problem. I'm sure you'll find someone who needs a place to live and will be happy to work for their keep."

Faith opened her mouth to say she wished he'd mind his own business, but Gabe came into the kitchen just then.

"Did you tell her?" Gabe took the cup of coffee Faith handed him. "Thank you."

"About the advertisement he took upon himself to put in the papers?" At Gabe's nod, Faith sighed. "Yes, he told me."

"Good. If he hadn't done it, I most likely would have. You need help, Faith."

"So I've been told." She looked from one man to the other. "Several times today. I'll interview the applicants. And I'll pray about it."

"We can't ask for more than that, can we, Ben?"

"I'll be happy with that."

Faith shooed them in to breakfast. She supposed she should appreciate that they wanted her to have help. But she really didn't have time to interview people today. Still she prayed that the Lord would send the right person to become part of her household and that she would know her when she met her.

Faith dove into her work after breakfast, resigned to the fact that she'd be interrupted all day. But she was more than a little surprised when she opened the door midmorning to see a familiar face.

"Mrs. Lambert—oh, how wonderful it is to see you! I've been wondering if you made it all right." The older woman's spark seemed to have left her, but she smiled as Faith pulled her inside.

"Oh, my dear Faith. I had no idea this was your boarding-house. How lovely it is."

"How have you been? What can I do for you? I'm so glad you found us."

"Well to be truthful, dear, I've come to answer this advertisement."

Faith felt confused. Why would Mrs. Lambert need work? "I don't understand. Did you and Mr. Lambert not find a claim?"

"Oh, yes we did. It's not too far out of town. But. . ." Tears came to the older woman's eyes. "I lost my mister a little over a week ago. He just up and died on me."

"Oh. . ." Faith didn't know what to do but gather the woman into her arms. "I am so sorry. Please, come this way, and let me get you a cup of tea."

She led Mrs. Lambert down the hall and into the kitchen. "Please take a seat at the table, and let me make that tea."

"Thank you." Mrs. Lambert pulled a lace handkerchief from her sleeve and dabbed at her eyes. "I'm sorry. I just haven't known quite what to do. I brought him into town to have him buried, and I've been staying at the Hotel Carlton over on Harrison. I can't bring myself to go back home. And I don't know what to do about my place. But I can't farm it myself, and I just don't know what to do."

"You are more than welcome to stay here until you decide. We'll gather your things from the hotel this afternoon, and you'll stay right here with us."

"Faith dear, you are so nice. I'd love that. But only if you will let me work for my keep."

"But there's no need—"

"There is a need. You have one"—she waved the advertisement—"and I have one. I don't know what I'll do with the claim, but I can't go back to it right now, and I need work. I'd count it as a blessing if you'd hire me to help you. I can wash and clean with the best of them. And I'm not too bad a cook either. Please consider me for the position. Please just think about it."

Faith set a cup of tea in front of her and sat down with her own cup. She stirred her tea and shook her head. "I don't need to think about it. You have the position. I've been praying about it all morning, and the Lord answered my prayer more quickly than I ever imagined He would. He brought you to my door. Let's drink this tea, and I'll show you to your room."

Mrs. Lambert ducked her head and nodded, reaching out to pat Faith's hand. Faith knew she was trying to hide her tears, but there was no need. Faith brushed at her own. Mrs. Lambert would be part of this household for as long as she wanted to be.

❧

Mrs. Lambert had been quite pleased with the room Faith gave her. It was the last corner room upstairs, and Faith was glad she hadn't given it to any of the boarders. The sorrow in the woman's eyes broke Faith's heart.

She and her husband had made so many plans, and now. . . perhaps it was because Faith had had her own dreams shattered by the death of her husband that she could relate to what Mrs. Lambert was going through.

All Faith really knew was that the Lord knew what they both needed and brought Mrs. Lambert to her door. They decided that Ben and Matt would go back to the hotel with Mrs. Lambert to gather up her things, and she would start work the very next day.

But Faith wasn't surprised when Mrs. Lambert showed up in the kitchen right after supper with her apron on. She'd have protested, but it was a good time for the family to get to know her.

Matt and Hope remembered her from the day of the run, and Faith had never been more proud of them than she was at their response to seeing Mrs. Lambert again. Hope hugged her like a long-lost aunt, and Matt patted her shoulder at the news that her husband had passed away. Then they went to work cleaning up the kitchen so that Ben and Gabe could get to know Mrs. Lambert.

Faith poured them all some coffee and told of how Mrs. Lambert had convinced them all that they could make the trip without Ben.

"Lambert? Seems like I met him at the creek right before we all decided to go to the front of the line," Ben said. "I'm sure I did. I'm so sorry 'bout your loss, ma'am."

"Thank you. He was a good man. And he managed to get us a good stake. Built a little house already—we'd planned on adding on to it later. He got the crops planted, but I just don't see how I can keep it up by myself, and I don't take much to livin' out there all alone. I have a neighbor keepin' an eye on it until I get back out there, but at the time I thought I'd go right back." She shook her head. "I just can't bring myself to go."

"That's understandable," Gabe said.

"I'm just not sure what to do with the claim. My neighbor said he couldn't farm any more than he has right now, and even if he could, he can't afford to buy me out."

"You say it's not too far from town?" Ben asked.

"Well, it's about halfway between here and Edmond Station, I'd say."

"That's not bad." He exchanged a look with Faith before offering, "Would you like me to go take a look at it? I might can give you an idea what you could ask for it or if you could get someone to farm it for you."

"Oh, I don't want to impose on you. I'm sure you have your own work to do."

"It's not an imposition. I can ride out and be back in a day. Gabe won't mind."

"Not at all," Gabe added. "We're glad you answered Faith's advertisement. Be glad to help you any way we can."

"I'll take you up on your offer, then. It's a fine place, and I'll appreciate any advice you can give me."

"Maybe I'll go after church on Sunday and come back Monday morning. That way I won't miss that much time helping Gabe."

Faith was almost certain that Ben was looking for himself, but she didn't say anything. Mrs. Lambert needed advice, and Ben would know what to tell her.

"That won't be a problem. Take all the time you need," Gabe said.

"Thank you." Mrs. Lambert looked around the table. "I can't tell you how happy my husband would be to know I found Faith and you all. It means more to me than I can say to have a place, to be so welcomed here, and to have a family to care for. I thank the Lord for sending me here."

"No more than we thank Him for bringing you," Faith said. "I didn't much want to hire anyone. It was Ben's idea. But now I know that the Lord had a plan—probably from when we first met." She got up and hugged Mrs. Lambert's shoulders. "I'm so happy you are here with us. I hope we can be of some comfort to you. And I don't want you living out there by yourself either."

"Thank you. I can't tell you how I've worried about what I was going to do. But I should have known better. The Lord always takes care of His own." Mrs. Lambert took one last sip from her cup and carried it to the sink, where Hope took it from her.

"Thank you for everything. I'm going to call it a night now, but I'll be up to help you with breakfast first thing in the morning."

"You can sleep in—"

"No. I'll be awake early. I'll see you then."

Faith watched her leave the kitchen, blinking back tears. Then she shook her head and turned to her brother. "Thank you for placing that advertisement. Not so much for the help, but so that Mrs. Lambert would come to us."

"She sure is a nice lady," Hope said. "She made me feel better when I woke up that morning and found out Papa had left the night before."

"She made me feel like I could drive just as good as anyone," Matt added.

"And you did," Faith said. "She was an encourager for us all. Now I hope we can help her."

"You'll help her, Faith," Gabe said. "You nurture everyone."

# fourteen

Ben was more than pleased that the land was everything Mrs. Lambert had said it was. Bordering a creek, the site had a good water source, and her husband had known how to farm, no doubt about that. His rows lay long and straight, and everything looked good. But it did need taking care of, and Ben thought he might be the one to do it.

The house Lambert had built was small with just one bedroom, but it'd fit Ben's needs for now, especially if he let Matt and Hope stay with Faith. He knew Matt would rather be with him, but he did need his schooling. Molly would have insisted on it. He could work on adding a couple of bedrooms for the next summer. It was a prize piece of land, and he didn't want to let it get away—at least not until he was sure this was what he wanted.

Maybe he could convince Mrs. Lambert to let him farm it for her for a while. Long enough so that she was sure getting rid of it was what she wanted and for him to know for sure he wanted to be a farmer from now on.

The neighbor who'd been watching the place, John Barnett, said they'd had a little rain in the last week. Enough to give the crops a good watering, but Lambert had also dug a well and had an irrigation system of sorts going. Barnett said they'd helped each other dig the channels, and so far it was working well.

Barnett agreed to keep watch over it, and Ben told him he'd be sure to let him know what Mrs. Lambert was going to do. He headed back to Guthrie feeling as if *his* dream might be about to come true. And he didn't think Faith would be all that upset either. It was close enough to get into town whenever he needed to. Matt and Hope could come stay anytime they wanted to. He could even go help Gabe some.

He felt excitement mount the closer to town he got. He'd talk to Faith about it before he made an offer to Mrs. Lambert. But he felt sure Faith would support him. Especially as he wouldn't be that far away. Perhaps his time had come. He would pray and leave it in the Lord's hands. The Lord had taken good care of them so far. Ben had no doubt that He would continue to do so.

❧

Mrs. Lambert had insisted that Faith call her Rose, and so the family reciprocated and did away with the formalities. Matt and Hope called her Mrs. Rose, to show respect, but she'd already become part of the family to them all.

"I don't think I'd have lasted another month if you hadn't shown up, Rose," Faith said as they hung out the sheets they'd washed that morning. "I love running the boardinghouse, but I really gave no thought to all the work involved when I declared that was what I wanted to do. And it is what I want to do—but not without you."

Rose laughed. "You do my heart so good, Faith. It's me that wouldn't have lasted long without my Richard if I hadn't answered your advertisement. I'll miss him all the rest of my days, but I'll be able to live them full with the Lord's help and this family of yours."

True to her words, Rose could take care of a house with the best. And she was a very good cook. It'd been her idea for them to at least take turns cooking, to give Faith some rest.

They shared the workload, and Faith wasn't complaining. She only worried that Rose might be working too hard, but Rose assured her that it was just what she needed and definitely not too much work.

The boarders certainly had no complaints. If Faith couldn't get to their needs right away, Rose did.

"I've never felt so at home anywhere but my own home as I do now," Mrs. Warner had said just that morning. "It's not going to be easy to leave here. Maybe I could convince Mrs. Lambert to go with me."

When Faith told Rose what she had said, the older woman just huffed. "She'll not be able to do that. I'm here as long as you'll have me."

While everyone seemed to eat breakfast from the sideboard at different times of a morning and they all ate together at supper, the noon meal had become one where the boarders ate in the dining room and the family ate in the kitchen. If the men got to come home at all to eat, it was usually a quick meal, and they were dusty from work.

Faith enjoyed the noon meal as much as any because it, and their gathering before bedtime in the kitchen, seemed to be the only time they were able to visit and talk over their days. She was looking for Ben to show up anytime now from Rose's farm. Matt and Gabe arrived early, hoping he'd be back, too. Everyone was anxious to hear what he had to say.

But soon as Ben walked in the back door, Faith didn't have to ask. She could see from his smile and the shine in his eyes that her brother had found his dream.

Once the boarders were served, the family sat down to their meal of beans and cornbread. Faith asked Gabe to say the blessing, and he thanked the Lord for bringing Ben back safely and for all their many blessings, including the food they were about to eat.

"Well Ben, what did you think of my place?" Rose asked after he'd taken a bite or two.

"I think you have the prettiest place I've seen this side of heaven, Mrs. Rose."

Rose smiled at him and nodded. "My Richard used to say the very same thing."

"You won't have any problem selling it or farming it out. I'd like to think on it a bit, but I believe I have an answer to your dilemma that you might like. If it's all right with you, I'd like to mull it over a little longer before I put it before you."

"That's right fine with me, Ben. How were the neighbors?"

"Very nice. They are good people. John's been watching over your place and agreed to keep doing so for a while longer."

"That makes me feel better. I'd hate to see someone try to jump our claim."

"It'd be pretty hard to do with neighbors knowing what's going on. Try not to worry about that."

Faith listened to them talking, but she had a feeling she knew what her brother was going to offer Rose. She might as well accept that he'd be leaving before long. She looked at Matt and Hope, who seemed anxious to hear what their Papa had to say, too.

She hoped he'd agree to let them stay here so they could go to school, but all she could do was take it to the Lord. He knew what they all needed and had proved it over and over again.

❧

Ben sent Matt and Hope off to bed a little early that night, but he waited until Rose retired before he brought up the subject of her place to Faith and Gabe.

"Tell me what's on your mind, big brother, although I think I know what it is."

"You know me well, sis. And this isn't going to come as any surprise to you. Rose's place is surely one of the prettiest pieces of land I've ever seen. Lambert chose well. It's nestled in by a creek, has some nice trees on it, and the land is fertile as it comes. He's planted fruit trees that will be producing well in a few years and all kinds of vegetables coming up now. Looks like his cotton crop is going to be a good one, too. That man knew enough about farming that he has his own irrigation system going. Rose can get a high price for that land if she decides to sell it."

"You want it, don't you?"

"I think so. I know I don't want to let it get away from me. But what if she changes her mind in a few months or a year? It was her and her husband's dream. What I'm thinking is that maybe I could farm it for her. . . . She could pay me part of the profits. But that way, I'd be able to find out for sure if farming is something I really want to do, and she'd have time to decide if she really wants to sell out."

"That makes a lot of sense," Gabe said. "But what about Faith and the children?"

Faith shook her head and smiled at Gabe. "I've known this was what Ben wanted since the beginning of this adventure. He was kind enough to find me a place in town. I won't stop him from his dream."

"Thank you, Faith," Ben said. "I knew you'd support me."

"What about Matt and Hope?"

"Well, I think I'll leave the decision to them. But the house is small, and I couldn't add on to it unless I buy it. It might be better for them to stay with you until I know for sure what I'm going to do anyway." He turned to Gabe. "You'll watch over my family, won't you?"

Faith found herself holding her breath, waiting for Gabe's answer. She didn't have to wait long.

"You know I will. I guess I just didn't know you wanted to farm so badly."

Ben shrugged. "It wasn't anything I thought I'd be doing quite this soon. I wanted to see Faith settled and happy first. But it looks like the boardinghouse is going to do real well, and while I do like working with you, I need to try this."

"I can understand that."

Faith looked over to find Gabe's gaze on her, and her heart set to beating double time. All the man had to do was look at her, and her pulse began to race.

"I'll take good care of them," Gabe said. "That I can promise you. But first there are a few things I need to tell you about me. You might not be so eager for me to watch over yours once you know."

His tone was so solemn that Faith's heartbeat seemed to come to a standstill.

"That sounds serous. Faith, pour us some more coffee, and we'll hear what Gabe has to say."

ᚥ

Gabe had known this talk was coming for some time now. He could find no way around it. It was time to let Ben and Faith know about his past.

"I can tell you that this new start here in Guthrie is one I desperately needed. I had a thriving business in Wichita, building homes and businesses much like here. But then the economic collapse came along and about did that in. . .and put a hold on my impending marriage. Before we could set another date, my fiancée was killed in a bank robbery."

He could hear Faith's quick intake of breath before she

said, "I'm so sorry, Gabe."

He took the hand she held out to him and squeezed it. For a moment he was at a loss for words, and even if he'd had them, he didn't think they'd come out for the lump in his throat. He nodded and took a sip of coffee before continuing, "Something happened to me when my fiancée was killed. The robber got away, and it became my obsession to find him to make sure he paid for what he'd done."

"I think I can understand that," Ben said.

Gabe shook his head. "I was grieving so badly, I couldn't think of anything but finding him. For a year I searched, going from one town to another. Finally when I'd about given up hope, I found him in El Dorado. It ended in a gun fight."

"Did you. . . ? Did you—"

"No, Faith. I didn't kill him. But he shot at me, and I shot back. I wounded him. And I spent more than a few months in jail until a trial proved that he was indeed my fiancée's murderer."

He could hear the *swoosh* of the breath Faith had been holding. "I just wanted you to know in case someone ever tells you they met me in jail. They could well be telling the truth. I probably should have let the law handle it from the first. Finding him didn't bring Laura back. And I wouldn't have a past I can't deny."

"But you were cleared, Gabe," Faith said.

"That's true. But it doesn't change the fact that I've spent time behind bars. I committed a crime, too."

"Well, in self-defense, I'm not sure that is true. But if so, you did your time. It's over."

"Maybe. Maybe not," Gabe said. "But because I left town looking for Jack Morrow, somehow some people thought

I was connected to the crime. I found out later there was a wanted poster with my face on it out there. I think that's what worries me the most. There are always people out there that try to cause trouble."

"You can't live your life worrying about that, Gabe."

"I know. I just wanted you to know in case—"

"There is no 'in case,'" Ben stated. "We've known what kind of man you are from the day we met you. You came to our aid without being asked. You've come to my defense; you've built Faith this home—you're the kind of man I trust to watch over my family. Can't think of anyone I'd trust more."

"Neither would I," Faith said softly.

Gabe's relief whooshed out loudly, causing Ben to chuckle and Faith to smile. But the look in her eyes was caring, and he finally felt peace about what he'd been so afraid to say to them. "Thank you. I can't tell you what that means to me. I'll take care of your family, Ben."

"I know you will."

"And I know I'll feel safer knowing you are here with Ben gone," Faith said. "Thank you, Gabe."

His heart did some funny kind of jump at Faith's soft words. "No. Thank you. For believing in me, for trusting in me, and for counting on me. I guess I'll go on up. You two probably have things to discuss. When do you think you'll be leaving, Ben?"

"I'm going to help you finish the Littletons' home. I can go to the farm on the weekends and come back. I'm sure the neighbor will watch things for a few more weeks once he knows someone is coming to take care of it."

"You don't have to do that. Matt will be here."

"I know. But I want to help. I'll run it by Rose and see

what she says though."

"Just let me know. But whatever you decide is fine with me. Goodnight."

"Goodnight, Gabe. Sleep well."

"You, too." Gabe left the brother and sister to talk about Ben's plans and headed up to his room. He loved the way Faith had started telling him to sleep well. He seemed to sleep better because of it.

It felt so good to get it all off his chest—if he'd known how they would have reacted to his story, he would have told them long ago. Finally he might be able to put his past behind and get on with his life. A life that he wanted to share with Faith. Now that he'd told her about his past, could there be a chance for them? Or would he be bringing her a mess of problems that couldn't be foreseen?

# fifteen

True to his word, Ben helped get most of the work done on the Littleton place before he took off. Rose was happy with whatever he wanted to do, but they settled for him working the farm for her at least until after harvest. Then they'd make up their minds about what to do.

Gabe continued to make sure Faith had all she needed. He and Matt split firewood and kept plenty stacked near the kitchen. He checked the water reservoir every time he came into the kitchen, and that was fairly often.

Faith had come to look forward to the time after her boarders had gone up for the evening while just she and Rose cleaned up. Gabe would come in and ask for a last cup of coffee or something cool to drink.

Her pulse began to race now as she heard his footsteps in the hall, just after Rose went up to her room.

"Got some coffee left?" he asked as he entered the kitchen.

"I do." She poured a cup and handed it to him. "How is work going on the Johnson house?"

"It's coming along real good. Matt's been a lot of help."

"It's going to be very pretty, but I still like mine the best."

Gabe smiled at her. "I'm glad. I wouldn't want you to be wishing you'd picked another plan."

Faith joined him at the table, bringing a plate of sugar cookies with her. "I don't think you could draw up a plan I'd like any better."

"I hope not. How was your day?"

"Busy as usual. But I love running the boardinghouse even better than I thought I would. I'm tired at the end of a day, but it's a good tired."

"It's a blessing to love what you do, isn't it?"

Faith nodded. She felt blessed in all kinds of ways these days. And one of those blessings was sitting right across the table from her. The more time she spent with Gabe, the more she wanted to be with him, and Faith had come to realize that she could no more stop her growing feelings for him than she could give up breathing. But she couldn't let him know how she felt. One day she'd have to watch him fall in love and marry another—someone who could give him a child. But knowing all that didn't stop her heart from beating faster each time she turned to see him watching her. Or her pulse from racing when he came near or gave her a smile, just as it was doing now.

She looked forward to seeing him come into the kitchen each morning and telling him goodnight each evening. He'd stopped talking about building his apartment—in fact he hadn't mentioned it since Ben had left, and she hoped he didn't start. She felt safe with Gabe in the house, and she couldn't quite imagine him not being there. Didn't want to even think about it, although she knew that day would come. *But not yet. Please, dear Lord, not yet.*

Life was good, and she was enjoying each day. The boarders were fairly easy to care for, and all of them seemed to be becoming real friends. With Rose's help, she wasn't exhausted at the end of a day. She missed Ben, but other than that, life was good.

The only thing that would make it better was a dream that couldn't be, so she'd be thankful for what she had and try not to get lost in that dream.

ta

Several weeks later, as the heat of summer began to give way to crisp days of fall, Faith was still counting her blessings. Ben had come in for the weekend, and they'd had a wonderful time. She'd made his favorite meals, and he'd taken Matt and Hope back with him for the week.

Guthrie continued to grow and change. Guthrie's school board, along with the boards of the other three cities—East and West Guthrie and Capitol Hill—joined to provide a consolidated school system. Classes would commence on October 14. Late to be sure, but at least they had a public school system in place.

Until then, Matt and Hope would alternate weeks staying with Ben on the farm and with Hope in town. They had made friends with several young people their own age and were looking forward to the start of school.

Faith had just finished a cup of tea after hanging out the sheets she and Rose had washed earlier that morning, when someone banged on the back door.

Rose hurried to answer it, and when she swung the door open, Faith's stomach turned. She began to tremble. Frank Jarvis had come back.

"I want ta see Ben Thompson," he said.

"He's not here right now."

Faith hurried to the door. "It's all right, Rose. I'll talk to the man."

"Thought you'd seen the last of me, didn't you, missy? I told ya I'd be back. Now where's that brother of yours?"

"He's working right now. Can I give him a message?"

"I reckon you can. You can tell him I'm back, and I intend to get what's mine. You can put up all the fancy buildings you want to, but there goin' ta be mine. I'm goin' to the land office now to tell 'em about your brother. You can tell him he can find me there." He turned and stomped off.

"Who is that man? I don't much like his attitude," Rose said, her hands on her hips.

"Then your instincts are good, Rose. He's here to cause problems. He tried to say Ben had come into Guthrie early and claimed his lot. Then when everyone around us came to Ben's defense, he just seemed to disappear. But I've always been afraid he'd come back."

"Well, you were right."

"I've got to find Gabe. Will you be all right here?"

"I'll be fine. I won't open the door if he comes back. And I have my pistol upstairs. I'll go get it."

Faith waited to leave until Rose came back down. She didn't know if Jarvis was serious about going to the land office or not, but she needed to tell Gabe what he'd said. Gabe would know what to do. She prayed he would. And she thanked the Lord that Ben had taken Matt and Hope to the farm. She walked as fast as she could down the street to where Gabe was working. Ordinarily she'd enjoy watching work on the house, but today she hurried up to him. "Gabe!"

He turned, "What is it, Faith? What's wrong?"

"Jarvis. He's back, and he said he was going to the land office—that he was going to tell them again about Ben taking his claim. I'm not sure that man is right in his mind, Gabe."

"Neither am I. But try not to worry. I'll go to the land office myself and find out what he's up to. I'll make sure you get home safely first though."

Faith started to protest and then changed her mind. She'd been looking behind her all the way here, afraid he might be following her.

Once they were back at the boardinghouse, she turned to him. "I hate to pull you into all this, Gabe, but with Ben gone, I didn't know what else to do."

"You did the right thing. You and Rose stay inside, and I'll be back soon as I can be."

Faith watched him leave, praying that Jarvis wasn't hiding out somewhere, waiting for Gabe.

❧

Gabe wasn't surprised by the fact that Jarvis had come back. He'd been expecting him to. Like Faith, he wasn't sure the man was right in the head, but one thing he was certain of was that Jarvis could cause problems for all of them.

When Gabe showed up at the land office, Jarvis was yelling at the agent, saying that Ben Thompson had stolen his lot months ago. When he spotted Gabe, he yelled out, "And that there man is tryin' to grab the claim out from under Thompson by rentin' a room at the boardinghouse Thompson's sister runs. He wants that land himself now it's got improvements on it!"

"That's ridiculous, Jarvis. I have my own claim."

"You're a lyin' just like you did that first day."

"I'm not lying, Jarvis. Besides, the claim you are talking about isn't Ben's. It's his sister's, and she came in later than we did."

That seemed to take the wind out of the man's sails. "Why. . .why that ain't true," he sputtered.

"It is true, and we can prove it. No one stole your claim. Now quit accusing us of it, or I'm going to the marshal's office and have him arrest you for threatening Mrs. Anderson."

"You ain't gonna do that, Logan." Jarvis cackled. "I know you ain't. And you haven't heard the last from me yet."

With that, he turned and walked out.

"Guess he's done accusing for today," the agent said. "You kind of knocked all the air right out of him. Good thing, too. I'm gettin' real tired of hearin' his accusations."

"Does he make them often?"

"About once a month. He says one of those lots over on First Street is his. Trouble is, he really can't prove a thing. But he is convinced he's been done wrong, and he intends to set it right. Just be on guard. He's kind of like a loose cannon."

"I couldn't have said it better myself. And that's the part that's scary." Gabe shook his head and left the office. On one hand, it seemed the agent knew Jarvis wasn't quite stable. On the other hand, there didn't seem to be a thing one could do about it. Loose cannon was right.

When he got back to the boardinghouse, Gabe was relieved that Jarvis hadn't been back, and he told the women to keep their pistols handy just in case.

He went back to work, glad he was working just down the street. He wished Matt hadn't gone to the farm. He could have left him on guard at the boardinghouse. The kid was a good shot, and much as Gabe never wanted to have to use his gun again, he wouldn't hesitate when it came to protecting those he cared about.

It wasn't until after supper that Gabe had a chance to talk to Faith alone. He found her outside, taking laundry off the line. It was still light outside, but the sun was setting. Soon it would be twilight. His favorite time of day.

She looked around when she heard his footsteps and put a hand to her heart. "Oh Gabe. It's you. I—"

"I'm sorry, Faith. I should have called out, especially after today."

"Did you want a cup of coffee? I'm going to put a fresh pot on when I go inside."

Gabe shook his head. The woman was always thinking about someone else. "No, I came to find you. I just wanted to see how you are. I'm sure that was nerve-wracking to have Jarvis show up like he did."

"It rattled me a little to be sure. But once you came back and told me what happened at the land office, I felt better. I don't know what's going on with that man, but I really don't believe he can get my place."

"There's no way I'd let him do that, Faith."

She sighed and looked away. "I know. Thank you for being there today." Her voice sounded funny as she continued. "Thanks for going to the land office and. . ."

Gabe turned her toward him only to see tears in her eyes and one beginning to slide down her cheek. She seemed to swallow a sob as she went on. "Thank you for helping."

He'd never seen Faith cry, and it was his undoing. He pulled her close, and she began to sob in earnest. "Please don't cry, Faith. I won't let him hurt you or take your land or—"

"I. . .know. I just, oh Gabe, I'm so thankful Matt and Hope aren't here. What if he does try to cause trouble? I don't want them hurt."

Gabe tipped her face up and found her eyes swimming in tears, yet there was a fierce look in them. He suddenly knew without a doubt that she'd use her pistol before she let Jarvis or anyone else hurt anyone she cared about. She might have tears in her eyes, but Faith Anderson was one of the strongest women he'd ever met. And he loved her with all his heart.

He tipped her chin higher, leaned down, and kissed the lips he'd loved to look at for so long. They were soft and supple, just as he knew they would be. And his heart seemed to turn to mush as they pressed against his. . .and clung.

"Faith? Faith are you out here?" Rose called from the back porch.

Faith jerked away and took a deep breath before realizing they were behind the last sheet on the line and Rose couldn't see them.

Gabe released a sigh of relief at the same time Faith did. The last thing he wanted to do was cause her embarrassment.

"I'm here, Rose. Gabe is helping me bring in the laundry. I'll be right there."

She looked up at Gabe, and he was glad to see the tears had been replaced by a different kind of sheen. "I'd better go put that coffee on," she whispered. "Would you bring in the basket?"

"I'd be glad to." Gabe took down the last sheet and watched her hurry inside. He hadn't imagined her response. She'd kissed him back. He looked up at the twilight sky he loved. Dark in the east, deep blue above, and shades of all kinds of mauve, pink, and yellow settling into the sun that was just disappearing over the horizon. He'd never see twilight again without remembering that kiss.

&

Faith seemed flustered the rest of the evening. Each time she looked at Gabe, a delicate flush colored her cheeks, and he wondered if she was still thinking about the kiss they'd shared. He certainly was. He had a feeling she didn't want to talk about it, but he certainly hoped she didn't regret it.

He went out and gathered kindling to add to the wood box he'd filled after bringing in the laundry. Rose was busy at the table, folding the sheet he and Faith had shared the kiss behind. She might not have seen them, but she seemed to sense that something was different between the two of them. When Faith wasn't looking, she raised an eyebrow in Gabe's direction as if she was asking what was going on.

He only smiled and shrugged, but he could feel his earlobes getting warm. Rose just grinned and actually winked at him. For some reason, he felt she'd given her approval to how he felt about Faith.

The older woman had been watching them for weeks now. She hadn't been born yesterday, and Gabe was pretty sure she knew he was in love with Faith. Or suspected it at the very least.

For the first time, he began to hope that he might be able to have a future with Faith. She knew about his past, and still she'd kissed him back. Was it possible she cared about him, too? But even if she did, could he ask her to marry him, knowing about his past and sure that any children they might have would find out, too? What would that do to them?

By the time Gabe went up to bed, he was more confused than ever. The only thing he knew to do was to ask the Lord for guidance, and so he did.

"Dear Lord, I never thought I'd love anyone after Laura died. But Faith is. . .well, You know Faith better than I do, Lord. You know that she is loving and nurturing, that she loves You and is faithful to You. She is a shining example of her name. She's touched my heart in ways that no one else has. Not even Laura. I don't want to bring her or her family any distress because of I spent time behind bars. Because there might still be wanted posters out there for me to cause problems down the road. But I love her, Father. Please guide me. Help me know what to do. In Jesus' name. Amen."

## sixteen

Faith went through the next few days full of mixed emotions. She relived the kiss with Gabe over and over again. She had no need to pinch her cheeks to bring a little color to them. All she had to do was remember his lips on hers—and that happened every time she caught him looking at her.

She felt flustered most of the time, wondering what he must think of her returning his kiss the way she did, chastising herself for even letting it happen, and yet wishing it would happen again.

Up and down her emotions went. She was almost certain that Gabe cared about her the same way she cared about him. But that would all change if he ever found out she couldn't give him children, and she didn't think she could bear to see that look of disappointment in his eyes.

By Thursday, she was still dreaming about that moment in her backyard. . .and praying for the Lord to help her distance herself from Gabe. Praying for strength so that she could accept it when Gabe found someone to love and have a family with.

"Is Ben coming in this weekend?"

Startled to hear Gabe's voice right behind her, Faith turned from stirring the soup she'd put on earlier. Had she spoken any of her thoughts out loud? Oh, she hoped not. "Gabe, I didn't hear you come in."

"You were deep in thought. Should I ask if you'll take a penny for them?"

"No." Faith turned back to the soup, hoping he'd attribute the warmth spreading up her neck and face to the heat from the range. "As far as I know, Ben is coming into town. He said they'd be here Friday."

"Good." Gabe sighed. "We haven't seen the last of Jarvis. The marshal came by today. He said Jarvis is making such a pest of himself, we've got to have a hearing before the arbitration board. It's set for next Monday."

"Ben should probably be there." Faith felt dread deep in her stomach. "I can't believe they're even going to listen to that man."

"It's probably best to get a hearing over with and settle it once and for all."

"But what if they decide—"

"Let's not think that way, Faith. We'll pray about it and leave it in the Lord's hands. I didn't want to have to tell you, but I needed to know if Ben was going to be coming home or if I needed to go get him."

"Do you think we should have him take Matt and Hope back with him?"

"I don't know. We need to tell him about Jarvis and let him decide, I suppose." Gabe reached out, grabbed the coffee pot, and poured himself a cup.

His nearness had Faith catching her breath at the fierceness of her beating heart. She had to get her feelings under control—soon. "Yes. He should be the one to make the decision. In the meantime, I'll pray that all this can be settled once and for all so Jarvis doesn't bother us anymore."

Gabe took a seat at the table. "You know, I was talking to John Littleton the other day, and he said he saw Jarvis making the same charge against the man whose claim was in the middle of the street. Remember him?"

"I do. Can't say I blame him for being upset about having to give up his claim. They sure didn't make it clear where the streets were." Faith tasted the soup and added a little more salt and pepper to it.

"No, they didn't. I feel sorry for all of those folks who had to be evicted."

"At least they'd come in and put claim to them. I'm not sure Jarvis even knew which claim he thought had been stolen."

"Probably because he didn't have a claim to steal. I believe he was just tryin' to get one in a mighty roundabout way."

Rose entered the kitchen just then. "I couldn't help but overhear. Are y'all talking about that crazy man who came by the other day?"

"Yes."

"I thought so. He's up to no good if ever a man was."

"Yes, he is."

Gabe filled Rose in on what was happening.

"I'll be praying everything turns out fine. Surely no one is going to believe him."

There didn't seem to be anything else to say, and Faith decided it was time for a change of subject. "I hate for Ben, Matt, and Hope to have to come home to this news, but I'll sure be glad to see them. I've missed them sorely."

"Well, I can tell you, I'll be glad to see those young'uns again. They sure bring life to a household," Rose said.

"They do. It's been awfully quiet around here, hasn't it?" Faith was thankful for Rose's assistance in getting the conversation around to a happier topic. She didn't want to think about Jarvis again tonight. And she missed the sound of Matt's and Hope's footsteps running up and down the stairs. Everyone else went at a much slower pace, but those two fairly flew down the stairs. She missed talking to them and even hearing the occasional argument they got into.

"Well, I've missed them, too," Gabe admitted. "Hope's smile is pure sunshine, and Matt is one good worker. I'm sure Ben would like to keep them out there with him."

"I told him he could go ahead and build an extra bedroom or two onto the house, but he said he'd wait until he knew for sure what he wanted to do," Rose said.

"Maybe he'll know when he comes home. I'll just be glad to see them all."

Rose called it a night and left Faith and Gabe in the kitchen.

Faith washed their cups and the coffee pot and was a little surprised when Gabe took up a dishtowel and began to dry.

"I'm sorry I had to put a damper on your evening by bringing up Jarvis again."

"I had to know," Faith said. She felt a little breathless as she shared the household chore with Gabe.

"It's going to be all right."

"I hope so." She looked up at him and found that his gaze was on her lips. Hers strayed to his. All thought of Jarvis vanished as memories of Gabe's kiss filled the space between them.

Gabe's hand touched her arm, and Faith caught her breath as his head dipped toward hers. . .ever closer. . .his lips softly touching hers. Faith stood on tiptoe—

"Miss Anderson, are you still up?"

At the sound of Mrs. Warner's voice, Faith and Gabe broke apart and backed up a few steps just before the woman peeked her head around the door.

"Miss Anderson, I was wondering if I could take my

husband up a glass of warm milk. He's having trouble getting to sleep."

"Of course. I'll heat some up right away."

Gabe still held the dishtowel in his hand, and Faith gently pulled it from his grasp. "Thank you for helping."

"You're welcome. I guess I'll call it a day. Mrs. Warner, I hope that milk helps your husband."

"Thank you, Mr. Logan. I'm sure it will."

Gabe turned back to Faith, "Goodnight."

"Goodnight, Gabe. Sleep well."

"You, too."

Faith busied herself getting the milk ready for Mrs. Warner to take to her husband. It was a good thing she'd interrupted them. Otherwise, Faith would surely have had two kisses to try to forget, and one was plenty. . .although she'd longed for another.

Soon as Mrs. Warner left the kitchen, Faith washed up the pan she'd heated the milk in and headed to her room. She was so thankful tomorrow was Friday. With Ben and his children in the house, maybe she'd be able to stay so busy she could put that kiss behind her and stop dreaming about the impossible.

❧

Faith spent all morning the next day preparing her family's favorites to celebrate their homecoming. For Matt, she made the oatmeal cookies he loved; for Ben, she prepared apple pies; and for Hope, she made a three-layer chocolate cake. With boarders in the house, it would all be eaten, but she'd make sure that her family got the first piece of their favorite dessert.

She and Rose had cleaned and aired out their rooms the day before, and now Faith pulled out the huge beef roast she'd had in the oven since noon. The dutch oven was filled with potatoes, onions, and carrots, and the meat was cooked fork tender. The dining room table was set and ready, and all they were waiting for was Ben and his children to come in the door.

Even the boarders seemed excited to see them.

"I've missed those children," Mrs. Fairmont said. "One thing I love about this boardinghouse is that it has those young people. And they are so nice and polite. Matt is always good to help me get my shopping bags up the stairs, and Hope loves to let me show her my purchases."

"Oh, I feel the same way," Mrs. Warner said. "They remind me of my niece and nephew back home. They keep me from missing them quite so much."

It did Faith's heart good to hear that her boarders liked having her family around. Perhaps it was why they thought her boardinghouse had such a homey feel to it. But no one was happier to see her family walk in the door than she was.

Supper was quite a homecoming all the way around as conversation flowed about what was going on in town, how the crops were doing on Rose's farm, and the changes Ben thought he might want to make. They all lingered at the table after dessert, just enjoying having everyone together again.

But it wasn't until the boarders had gone upstairs and the family gathered in the kitchen that Faith felt that her brother, niece, and nephew were really home. It was then that they filled Ben in on Jarvis's visit, the accusations he'd leveled at Ben and then Gabe, and about the hearing set for Monday.

"You do seem to be off the hook now, Ben. Once he found out that the claim isn't yours but Faith's, he turned his focus on me, claiming I was after this claim."

"That old man is crazy," Matt said.

"He might be. And that's part of the problem," Gabe said. "There's no telling what he's going to do next."

"You know, I still think I've seen him before," Ben said. "His face is so familiar to me. . . ."

"Well, much as I've missed you all, I'm glad Matt and Hope were with you. Maybe you'd better take them back to the farm until after the hearing," Faith said.

"No. I'm not going anywhere until after that hearing. Jarvis isn't going to take either of your claims."

"Wish we could find out where he came from or something about his past," Gabe said. "Maybe the marshal can—"

Ben jumped up from the table. "I know where I saw him! Right after we got to Arkansas City, I saw a man running out of a dry goods store with a bag in his hands. A clerk came running out behind him saying the store had been robbed, but by then the man had disappeared. I'm almost certain that man is Jarvis."

"Which might explain why he accused you of taking his claim. He was hoping to get rid of you before you remembered him," Gabe said.

Ben shook his head. "I don't know about that. He was in such a hurry, he probably didn't even see me."

"Well," Rose suggested, "maybe he buried the money he stole on the lot and—"

"That well could be it, Mrs. Rose. He wanted the lot so he could get to the money," Ben said.

Faith nodded. "It makes sense if he's the man Ben saw in Arkansas City."

"We'll go see the marshal first thing in the morning. He has to know about Jarvis before the hearing," Gabe said. "One never knows about the boards and how they make their decisions. Getting to the bottom of why Jarvis wants these lots may be the only way to settle this thing."

❧

Gabe and Ben left the house right after breakfast the next morning. Gabe was relieved that Ben was home. Surely between the two of them they could make sure Faith kept her claim.

"How has Faith been?" Ben asked. "Did Jarvis's visit upset her too much?"

Gabe shook his head and tried to clear the memory of his and Faith's kiss that just the mention of Jarvis always brought to mind. "She handled it very well, but she was glad Matt and Hope weren't here. She didn't know if Jarvis would try to hurt anyone or what was going to happen in the next day or two. Besides being beautiful inside and out, she's one strong woman, that sister of yours."

"Yes, she is. And as her big brother, is there something I should know about the two of you?"

Once more the kiss shot to Gabe's mind. "I can only tell you about me. I've come to care a great deal for Faith, but I. . .with my past and all. . ." He shook his head. "And I don't really know how she feels—"

"Gabe, are you saying you've fallen in love with my sister?"

Gabe grinned at his friend. "I believe I have."

"Well, tell me something I haven't suspected for a while. You two have been stealing glances at each other almost from the moment we met you."

"Well, I know how I feel, but I'm not sure about your sister."

"Maybe you should ask her."

By then they'd reached the marshal's office, but Gabe knew Ben wasn't done discussing Faith and that the subject would be sure to come up again.

"Good morning. What can I do for you two fellows?" The marshal welcomed them into his office.

They'd come to know each other better since Gabe's first visit, and it seemed to come as no surprise to the marshal that they were there about Frank Jarvis.

"I've heard he's tryin' to stir up trouble again."

"You heard right. And we think we may know why," Gabe said.

The marshal motioned for them to sit. "Tell me about it."

## seventeen

It was past noon when Gabe and Ben came back to the boardinghouse. Faith had served lunch for her boarders, and they'd taken off for town or to visit friends afterward. Matt and Hope had gone to visit friends, and Rose was resting upstairs before coming back down to help Faith start supper.

"Anything left to eat, sis?" Ben asked.

"I can make you a sandwich."

"That would be great."

Both men seemed much more relaxed than they had been when they left. "Thank you, Lord," Faith whispered as she fixed them each a sandwich from the leftover roast of the night before.

"We have a plan in place, but the marshal asked us to keep it quiet. He wants reactions to what might happen Monday to be genuine. But I think he's going to get to the bottom of it all," Gabe said.

"I sure hope so. It's one thing to be accused of something you've done. Another entirely to be accused of something you'd never do," Ben said. "I'd thought about staying out at the farm this weekend and sending word to you by one of the neighbors that might be coming in. But I'm sure glad we came on into town. I can't believe Jarvis can win this thing, but we need to keep in mind that if that should happen, the Lord will see us through."

"That's what I've been telling myself all day," Faith said.

"We've started over once; we can do it again with the Lord's help."

"We checked with a lawyer, and he said that if Jarvis is awarded the claim, he felt sure that he'll have to pay you something for the improvements that have been made," Gabe said.

"And I can't see how it could happen any other way," Ben said.

"Neither can I. Well, I'm going down the street to get some work done. Time passes faster when I'm busy."

"You're right about that. I'll be down to help out after I visit with Faith for a few minutes."

Gabe nodded. "See you then. Thank you for the lunch, Faith. We should have stopped and got something at a café instead of making more work for you."

"You're welcome, Gabe. It was no bother, really."

Gabe hesitated at the door for a moment and then opened it to go out. "See you later."

"See you later."

Faith turned to see her brother watching her closely, a smile on his face. She picked up his and Gabe's empty plates and took them over to the sink. "Want some coffee?" she asked, knowing what his answer would be and already pouring him a cup.

"Yeah, I'd like a cup if you'll sit with me for a bit."

"I'll be glad to take a break." She joined him at the table. "Besides, I want to hear how you like the farm and—"

"I want to talk to you about Gabe and your feelings for him."

"What are you talking about?" She'd just brought her cup to her lips, but her hands began to tremble, and she quickly returned it to its saucer.

"Faith, I've seen how the two of you look at each other.

You care about him. He cares about you. In fact, I think he's in love with you."

Faith's heart swelled to near bursting at her brother's words and then quickly deflated as if pricked with a pin. Unbidden tears gathered at the corners of her eyes. "It'd be best if he's not."

"Why? I know you care for Gabe. It's been clear to me since long before I ever went to the farm."

"You are right. I won't deny it. But nothing can ever come from it, Ben."

"Why not?"

Faith shook her head as tears she'd tried to hold back began to flow, and she brushed them with her hands. "No man is going to want to marry a woman who can't give him children. I saw the disappointment in Noah's eyes. I don't want to see it in Gabe's."

"Faith, I'm sorry. But if a man loves a woman, he can accept a lot of things. You didn't know you wouldn't have children when you married Noah, and he loved you anyway."

"But I saw that love change over time, and—"

"Faith, Gabe isn't Noah. If you love him and if he asks you to marry him, tell him what you've told me. Then let him decide."

"I don't know if I can bear to tell him. It'd just be better if he doesn't ask."

"I have a feeling he's going to ask, so you might as well be prepared for it. I love you, sis. I want you to be happy, and I think that can happen if you will allow Gabe to make his own decision about having children."

"He won't want me once he knows I can't have any."

"Don't make up his mind for him, Faith. Let *him* be the one to do that." Ben got up and kissed the top of her head. "Are you okay?"

At her nod and sniff, he said, "Trust that the Lord has a plan, sis. I'll see you later, okay?"

"Okay." Faith watched her brother go, thinking that she knew God had a plan. But she fully believed it was for her to accept the fact that she and Gabe weren't meant to be.

❧

In spite of Monday's hearing looming over their thoughts, they managed to have a wonderful Lord's Day. It was good to be in church together—the sermon seemed meant just for them. It was taken from Psalm 56:3 and talked about putting one's trust in the Lord when one was afraid. It went straight to Faith's heart. She'd been afraid of so much in the last few days. Perhaps she hadn't trusted the Lord for the outcome the way she should. By the time the service was over, Faith was determined to turn her worries over to the Lord.

She'd put a ham on early that morning, and it was done to perfection for Sunday dinner. Several trees at the back of the lot gave good shade, and Gabe and Ben set up a croquet course under their branches. Everyone took a turn playing later in the day when it cooled off a bit.

Somehow word had gotten around that someone was causing problems for Faith and Gabe, and her boarders were a little concerned about what would happen if Jarvis won his case, yet they were very supportive, asking if they could do anything to help.

"Thank you so much. We'd appreciate your prayers," Faith said. "It's all in the Lord's hands now. Hopefully it will all be settled tomorrow."

"Well, I'm going to give my witness if needed," Rose said. "I know when you came in to town, and they aren't about to find you guilty of coming in and jumping a claim if I have anything to do with it."

Faith bent down and hugged the woman, who'd just brought out a pitcher of lemonade. "Thank you for all the support you give me, Rose."

She'd come to love Rose like a mother. She felt blessed that the Lord had led her to them.

By the time she went to bed that night, Faith felt hopeful that things would turn out all right, but she was ready to accept whatever happened the next day. She fell into a deep sleep, and it was only hearing a commotion outside her window that woke her the next morning. The sun was barely up when she looked out the window to find men swarming her lot with picks and shovels. She threw on her clothes and hurried outside to find Ben and Gabe already sipping coffee and watching her yard being torn up.

"What is going on here? Ben? Gabe? Why are you sitting here letting these men dig up my yard?"

"Don't have much choice, Faith," Gabe said. "Those are the marshal's people. They are looking for the money Jarvis may have buried back there."

"Oh. . ."

"Go grab a cup of coffee and join us."

"I don't have time for that. I have to make breakfast for the boarders."

"Well, will you bring ours out here?" Ben asked.

"Ben, we can go get it ourselves when it's ready," Gabe said. "Faith works hard enough as it is."

"Okay. Please call us when it's ready, sis," Ben grinned and winked at her.

Faith shook her head and sighed as she went back in to make breakfast. The hearing was set for one o'clock. She certainly hoped they found something before then, but from the piles of dirt outside, she was beginning to doubt that they would.

Just as she'd set everything out on the sideboard and rung the bell to tell her boarders breakfast was ready, there seemed to be more commotion outside, and she ran out to her porch.

"What is it this time?" But no one had to answer; she could see that the deputies had unearthed a box, and Jarvis seemed to have shown up out of nowhere.

"Why, Logan must have buried that there." He nodded at the marshal. "I told ya Logan was a crook!"

"Jarvis you'd better go easy on the accusations. We'll settle it all at the hearing," the marshal said. He nodded to two of his men. "You keep an eye on him and make sure he shows up at one o'clock sharp."

"Yes, sir."

The marshal tipped his hat to Faith. "Mornin', ma'am. Sorry to mess up your yard. I'll make sure my men put it back the way it was. See you after awhile."

Faith only nodded. She didn't know whether to be relieved or frightened about what was going to happen at the hearing, so she closed her eyes and sent up a silent prayer. *"Dear Lord, please be with us today, please let the truth come out, and please let us keep our claims. Especially Gabe, Lord. He's done so much for us, been there whenever we've needed him. And I love him, Lord. He's already suffered so much sorrow. Please don't let him suffer more. Thank You for everything, most especially for Your Son and our Savior. It is in His name I pray. Amen."*

❧

By the time the hearing got underway, there was standing room only. Jarvis made his claim, but when asked where his witnesses were, he could call on no one. "That don't mean anythin'. I put claim to that lot where sits that boarding-house. It's rightly mine."

"This isn't the first time you've made that claim, Jarvis. But it's time to put a stop to it one way or another," the register of deeds said.

Faith was questioned first.

"To your knowledge, Miss Anderson, when did your brother come in to Guthrie?"

"He left camp the night before the run to go to the front of the line," Faith said truthfully. "And I know my brother, sir. He would not have come in early."

"And when did you come in?"

"I got here late on the twenty-second. So many people were here I had trouble finding my brother."

"And is there anyone who can witness that?"

Rose stood up. "I can, sir. Faith and her niece and nephew left camp the same time I did. As soon as that gun went off on the twenty-second."

"And Gabe Logan. When did he come in?"

"I don't know that, sir. He wasn't with us."

"He came in with me," Ben said. "We were on the front of the line, and we took off about the same time when the gunshot went off to let us know we could. We reined in on our lots at the same time."

"Do you have any other witnesses to that?"

"He does," a man from the back of the room said. "I read about this in the paper and had to come. This Ben Thompson and Gabe Logan were at the front of the line with several others and me. Not one of us made a move before that gun went off."

"And who are you, sir?"

"I'm Jed Green. I met these fellows at the line. They took off like a shot once that gun went off. But not a minute before."

"Gabe Logan, when did you get into town?"

"I believe it was about midafternoon. Didn't look at my

watch. Didn't figure it mattered. But I can tell you true. No one I know came in early or jumped a claim. Ben and I went over every inch of those lots to make sure no one else had put a stake down."

"Is there anyone who can vouch for that?"

John Littleton came forward. "All I know is that I was there before these two men came in to town. And I never saw this Jarvis fellow until the next morning, when he accused Ben of stealing his lot. Now he's saying Gabe Logan stole his or wants Faith's. Which is it? He doesn't seem to know what lot he says he laid claim to. I can't believe we're even having a hearing on this."

"He's a lyin', too," Jarvis yelled. "All these people are friends. They'd say anything to help each other. And Logan would say anything to help Thompson's sister. He wants that lot for himself."

"I have a lot, Jarvis. I don't need Miss Anderson's."

"But that's where you hid the money you stole in Arkansas City! That there box they found today is proof he's a criminal like I told you, Marshal. When are you gonna arrest him?"

Total silence fell on the room as everyone waited for the marshal's answer.

"Jarvis, there's only one way you could know Gabe stole that money. And that's if you saw him do it."

"I did! I've been telling you that."

"In Arkansas City on the 10th of November of last year?"

"That's right."

"Well Jarvis, it appears to me that *you* are the liar. There is no way you could have witnessed Mr. Logan robbing that dry goods store because he was in a jail in Wichita, Kansas, on that date for a crime he didn't commit. And I have proof of all that."

"Why—why. . ." Jarvis seemed at a loss for words.

"Furthermore," the marshal continued, "the only way you knew about the robbery and the location of the box that had been buried was because you were the one who robbed that store. And you are the one who came in early and buried that box. That's why you wanted that lot so bad. Deputies, arrest this man."

Jarvis tried to get away, but Gabe wrestled him to the ground before giving him over to the deputies. "Glad that's all settled, Jarvis. Now you can pay for your crime."

The register of deeds pounded his gavel. "This hearing will come to an end. Gabe Logan and Faith Anderson are the owners of the lots they've registered. There'll be no more hearings on this subject."

Ben gathered Faith and Gabe in a big hug, and everyone who'd come to help them came to congratulate them. Finally, it was over.

# eighteen

As they walked home, Gabe began to feel himself relax. Jarvis hadn't won. Gabe had kept his lot, and Faith would keep hers. Jarvis wouldn't cause them any more worry.

Faith turned to him. "Gabe, I'm so sorry your past had to come out like that. I'm sorry Jarvis made it necessary."

Gabe shrugged. "If I hadn't already told you and Ben, I'm not sure I'd have told the marshal he could get it all out in the open. But it's out there now, and I don't have to worry about someone coming into town and telling everyone about it. There's a lot of relief in that."

"I think we're all feeling relief tonight."

"I know I am," Ben said. "There's just not enough room out on Rose's farm for all of us." He grinned.

"I guess we could put up a barn," Rose said.

That got a chuckle from all of them.

"Thanks, Rose, but it'd be a little hard to run my business from your farm."

"I suppose."

When they arrived at the house, Ben's children were waiting on the front porch. "How did the hearing go?" Hope asked, running down the steps.

"It went real good. We keep our claims, and Jarvis serves some time," Faith said.

Matt, who was maturing faster than Faith was ready for, slapped his dad on the back and hugged Faith.

Hope hugged them both. "Oh, I'm so glad. I've been so

worried. We prayed and prayed."

"And that's what was needed. I know the Lord heard those prayers, and He answered them," Ben said.

"He certainly did," Faith added. "I think it's time for a celebration supper."

"I do, too, but you aren't going to cook it. I'm going to make it for you," Rose said. "Hope will help me. Won't you, dear?"

"I'd be glad to. I cooked out at the farm using some of Aunt Faith's recipes, and Papa said it was real good. Even Matt liked it."

"Well then, I think I'll go visit Amy and the baby and tell her to thank John for us again. I'll let you two get on with it," Faith said. "I'm just going to run in and freshen up, and I'll be on my way."

She turned and smiled at Gabe and Ben, her happiness glowing from her eyes. "I'll see you all later."

Rose and Hope went to make preparations for supper, and they talked Matt into running to the grocer's for them.

"Want me to come help you catch up on putting those walls up?" Ben asked.

"I'd like that," Gabe answered. "But first I'd like to talk to you about something. Come on over to my office, okay?"

"Sure."

In only a couple of minutes, they were sitting in Gabe's office, and he was trying to figure out how to bring up the subject uppermost on his mind.

"You going to get on with it, or are you expecting me to read your mind?" Ben said with a grin.

"You know what I want to say—ask, don't you?"

"I've got a good idea, but I need to hear it from you."

"I want your permission to ask Faith to marry me."

"You have it. But it's not me that you have to convince, my friend. It's Faith."

"I know. I'm praying she cares for me as much as I care for her."

"I believe she does. That isn't the problem."

"What is it then?"

"It's really not something I should tell you, but I don't want my sister hurt any more than she already has been. And I don't want you to ask her to marry you unless you can accept the reason she may tell you no."

Gabe's heart constricted in his chest. "Tell me."

"Faith wasn't able to have children when she was married to Noah. Of course she didn't know that she would not be able to give him a child when she married him, or she never would have. She says she'll never marry again because no man is going to want to marry a woman who can't give him children. And she can't bear the thought of disappointing another man."

Gabe was quiet, trying to take it all in. He'd always wanted children—until he'd spent time in jail, and then he'd wondered how they would feel, what they would think when they found out about his past. Even though he was innocent, it was a past he wasn't proud of.

He felt torn. He wasn't sure how he felt for himself about what Ben had just told him, but his heart ached for Faith. He'd seen her with the Littletons' baby. She loved children. Wanted one of her own badly.

"It's a lot to think about, I know. That's why I felt I had to tell you. Gabe, don't ask my sister to marry you unless you can accept the fact that you'll never have children."

❧

When Faith came back from the Littletons', Rose and Hope

wouldn't let her in the kitchen.

"Aunt Faith, we want to make a special supper for you."

"But I can—"

"Faith dear, Hope and I have this all planned out. Now you don't want to hurt our feelings, do you?" Rose said, putting an arm around Hope.

"You don't want to do that, do you, Aunt Faith?" Hope asked with a sparkle in her eyes.

"Of course not—"

"Then go on and relax and pretty yourself up. You can come back when we ring the bell for the boarders," Rose insisted.

Faith wasn't sure how she felt about not being allowed in her own kitchen, but she knew they were trying to give her a treat, so she decided to take her time getting dressed. It might be fun to act like one of her boarders.

She never had much time to pretty herself up before a meal. Trying to pin up an errant strand of hair was about it. She didn't even have to pinch her cheeks for color; if the range didn't provide it, one look at Gabe usually did.

Gabe. Her heart still hurt that his past had to come out the way it did. He'd suffered much in the last few years, as she had. And there'd be more to come for her. She loved the man. Loved him with all her heart. But after visiting with Amy and holding that precious child of hers, Faith knew she had to try to distance herself from Gabe.

For much as she loved him, she had to let him find someone else, someone who could give him children. She was going to have to accept the fact that she would have to watch Gabe Logan marry and have a family with another woman.

Faith caught her breath at the sharp pain that thought brought to her heart. She wasn't sure how she could stand it, but she had to. Gabe loved children as much as she did. She'd seen it numerous times in his actions with Matt and Hope and with any child who crossed his path. She'd even seen the same longing she felt in his eyes when he'd watched her holding little Lily.

Loving him was something she couldn't imagine not doing. But letting him know was something she must never do.

Her heart twisting with unshed tears, Faith began washing her face, finally letting the tears flow at the hopelessness of her feelings. Streaming down her face, her tears mixed with the water in the basin below.

*Dear Lord, please give me strength to distance myself from Gabe, to accept that I can't have a life with him, and to be happy for him when he finds someone to love.*

❧

Gabe got ready for the celebration supper Rose and Hope had planned with a prayer in his heart that, by the end of the evening, he would know what to do about Faith.

He and Ben had worked in silence after their talk, with Gabe going over all Ben had told him. Faith couldn't have children. Did it change the way he felt about her? No. Only in that his heart hurt for her and he wanted nothing more at that moment than to comfort her.

*But would that hold?* he'd asked himself. Could he ask Faith to marry him and truly accept that they'd never have a family? He'd never want to make her feel as if she was letting him down, and Ben was right. Unless he could accept her as she was and love her for the wonderful woman she was, he shouldn't, couldn't ask her to marry him.

When he'd gone back to his room, Gabe had taken all his concerns to the Lord. "Lord, I know I love Faith with all my heart, and I never want to hurt her. I admit I've dreamed of having a family with her, but I don't believe the possibility of having a family is why I fell in love with her. It's her, Faith, that makes my day brighter, that gives me hope for the future."

Gabe's heart twisted in pain at the very thought of not having Faith in his life. He just couldn't imagine it, not now. Not after seeking her sweet face first thing of a morning and waiting to hear her tell him to sleep well the last thing at night. What he wanted most was to be able to wake to that face each morning and kiss her goodnight before he went to sleep.

So he continued to pray, "Dear Lord, I believe I can be the husband Faith needs, with or without children in our lives. I believe I can accept that we'll never have children and love Faith more each day even without them. I want to ask her to marry me, to share our lives together. But only You know the future. If I cannot accept that it will just be the two of us for the rest of our lives, then please keep me from telling her how I feel. I do not want to hurt her in any way. I leave it in Your hands, Lord, and I thank You for all the blessings You've bestowed on me. Your will be done. In Jesus' name. Amen."

The supper bell rang, and Gabe went down to celebrate the victory over Jarvis with the others. He hoped that by the end of the evening he'd be celebrating something even more important to him.

Faith looked beautiful in a blue and yellow dress that brought out the red in her hair. His heart told him how much he loved her, and Gabe knew from the peace that stole over him the instant he saw her that he would ask her to marry him before the night was over.

Rose and Hope had gone all out, making fried chicken,

cream gravy, peas, and biscuits for the meal. They'd even made an apple pie for dessert. It was truly a celebration dinner, and everyone was overjoyed upon learning the results of the hearing.

"I can tell you, your family hasn't been the only ones praying," Mrs. Warner said. "Ida and I spent the whole time you were gone upstairs praying."

"Why thank you, Lottie and Ida. The Lord heard your prayers for sure," Faith said.

"Well, you've all become like family to us," Ida Fairmont said. "And we sure didn't know what we'd do if you lost this place. None of us are ready to move on, and some of us may never be."

"I can't tell you what that means to me—to all of us—to hear you say that. And we're so glad you are here to celebrate with us." Faith was touched at their words.

Conversation flowed over the meal and through the dessert, and Gabe was wondering if he'd ever get to talk to Faith alone. But finally everyone seemed ready to call it an evening, and he breathed a sigh of relief.

Still he wondered when his chance would come, but he didn't have to wait long. As if Rose read his mind, she held her hand up as Faith began to clear the table. "No. You aren't cleaning up either. Ben and Matt are going to help us. We've already come to an agreement on that. It's a beautiful evening. Go out on the porch for a spell, or take a walk and enjoy it."

"But I—"

"Gabe, take her outside please," Ben said.

"How about it, Faith? Want to sit a spell or take a walk?"

She hesitated only a moment. "I believe I'd like to take a walk."

He held out his arm, and she slipped her hand into the crook of his elbow. Gabe felt his chance had come, and he was going to make the most of it. They went outside and down the porch steps. "Which way? Over by the river or downtown?"

"How about both? Downtown first and then the river."

They strolled down First Street, with Faith commenting on first one and another lot that had changed in the few months they'd been there. "I can't believe the change in Guthrie. What was a sea of wagons and tents is fast becoming a real city."

"A year from now, we won't recognize it," Gabe said.

They turned down Oklahoma Avenue and headed toward Division Street. Many of the businesses were in frame buildings, and several brick buildings were going up.

They didn't talk much as they turned on Division and headed toward the river, but the silence was comfortable. And with each step that brought them closer to the river, Gabe knew what he wanted more and more.

It was getting close to twilight when they reached the riverbank, and after watching several people in rowboats fishing for a while, they started back to the boardinghouse.

"Would you sit with me for a moment?" Gabe motioned to the swing.

"I'd better not. I need to go get things started for breakfast."

Before he could object, she hurried inside. Gabe sighed. Well, he wasn't about to give up. Not now.

❦

Faith's heart hammered in her chest as she hurried to the kitchen and put on an apron. She had to distance herself from Gabe. Had to. She loved him more with each passing moment, and she shouldn't have gone on a walk with him.

The kitchen was spotless and empty. In fact, the whole

house seemed quieter than usual—except for the sound of Gabe's footsteps coming down the hall.

"Faith, please. I'd like to talk to you."

"Gabe, I—"

The man didn't give up. He walked over and took the bowl she'd just taken down from the cabinet out of her hands. He put it on the table and turned back to her. "Please?"

The look in his eyes shot straight into her heart. She'd never felt so shaky in her life, and she was afraid to speak. She could only nod.

"I've been wanting to tell you this for a while now. . ." Gabe walked toward her until he was standing a breath away. His arms came up on each side of her as if he thought she would bolt. He leaned his forehead on hers. "I love you with all my heart, Faith Anderson. I—do you think you could ever feel the same way about me?"

"No! Oh Gabe, it doesn't matter if I do or not. You mustn't love me. I. . . I'm not the woman for you."

"Yes, you are." He moved closer.

Faith held a hand to his chest and shook her head. She had to tell him. "No. I can't give you children, Gabe. I'm not the woman—"

His hands came up to cup her face as he looked into her eyes. "Faith Anderson, you are the only woman I love and the only one I want. Whether we can have children or not doesn't matter. I don't have the kind of past I'd want to tell my children about anyway."

"You'll come to regret it." And she didn't think she could bear it if he did.

Gabe shook his head. "No. I won't. I can live without children, but I don't want to spend my life without *you*. If it is the Lord's will that we not have children, so be it.

"You say that now, but—"

Gabe touched his fingers to her mouth. "I say that because it is true. All I truly want is you in my life for now and for always. I'll be content as long as you are by my side for the rest of my days. I love you, Faith. Please say you'll be my wife."

Faith's heart was so full of love for the man she couldn't find the right words to say. As she hesitated, Gabe gathered her in his arms and tipped her face to his.

"I love you, Faith. But if you say go away, I'll leave you alone, and I won't bother you again. The choice is yours."

Then his lips claimed hers in a kiss that told her just how much he loved her. And Faith responded, knowing that no matter where she lived, home was in Gabe Logan's arms.

When she finally drew back, Gabe whispered in her hair, "What's it to be, Faith? Will you marry me, or do I need to leave you alone?"

Faith stood on tiptoe and turned his face to hers. "Don't leave me alone. I'll marry you, Gabe Logan, because given my choices, I'd much sooner have love."

# A Letter To Our Readers

Dear Reader:

In order that we might better contribute to your reading enjoyment, we would appreciate your taking a few minutes to respond to the following questions. We welcome your comments and read each form and letter we receive. When completed, please return to the following:

Fiction Editor
Heartsong Presents
PO Box 719
Uhrichsville, Ohio 44683

1. Did you enjoy reading *I'd Sooner Have Love* by Janet Lee Barton?
   ❏ Very much! I would like to see more books by this author!
   ❏ Moderately. I would have enjoyed it more if

   _____

   _____

   _____

2. Are you a member of **Heartsong Presents**? ❏ Yes ❏ No
   If no, where did you purchase this book? _____

   _____

3. How would you rate, on a scale from 1 (poor) to 5 (superior), the cover design? _____

4. On a scale from 1 (poor) to 10 (superior), please rate the following elements.

   ____ Heroine          ____ Plot
   ____ Hero             ____ Inspirational theme
   ____ Setting          ____ Secondary characters

5. These characters were special because? _____
_____
_____

6. How has this book inspired your life? _____
_____
_____

7. What settings would you like to see covered in future
   **Heartsong Presents** books? _____
_____
_____

8. What are some inspirational themes you would like to see
   treated in future books? _____
_____
_____

9. Would you be interested in reading other **Heartsong
   Presents** titles? ❏ Yes ❏ No

10. Please check your age range:
    ❏ Under 18          ❏ 18-24
    ❏ 25-34             ❏ 35-45
    ❏ 46-55             ❏ Over 55

Name _____
Occupation _____
Address _____
City, State, Zip _____
E-mail _____

# Presents

## Great Inspirational Romance
## at a Great Price!

**Heartsong Presents** books are inspirational romances in contemporary and historical settings, designed to give you an enjoyable, spirit-lifting reading experience. You can choose wonderfully written titles from some of today's best authors like Wanda E. Brunstetter, Mary Connealy, Susan Page Davis, Cathy Marie Hake, Joyce Livingston, and many others.

*When ordering quantities less than six, above titles are $3.99 each.*
*Not all titles may be available at time of order.*

HEARTSONG
PRESENTS

# If you love Christian romance...

$12.<sup>99</sup>

You'll love Heartsong Presents' inspiring and faith-filled romances by today's very best Christian authors...Wanda E. Brunstetter, Mary Connealy, Susan Page Davis, Cathy Marie Hake, and Joyce Livingston, to mention a few!

When you join Heartsong Presents, you'll enjoy four brand-new, mass-market, 176-page books—two contemporary and two historical—that will build you up in your faith when you discover God's role in every relationship you read about!

Mass Market 176 Pages

Imagine. . .four new romances every four weeks—with men and women like you who long to meet the one God has chosen as the love of their lives…all for the low price of $12.99 postpaid.

To join, simply visit www.heartsong presents.com or complete the coupon below and mail it to the address provided.